WALTER SHERWOOD'S PROBATION

Horatio Alger, Jr.

1st WORLD
LIBRARY
Literary Society

Walter Sherwood's Probation

Horatio Alger, Jr.

© 1st World Library – Literary Society, 2005
PO Box 2211
Fairfield, IA 52556
www.1stworldlibrary.org
First Edition

LCCN: 2005906504

Softcover ISBN: 1-4218-1560-5
Hardcover ISBN: 1-4218-1460-9
eBook ISBN: 1-4218-1660-1

Purchase *"Walter Sherwood's Probation"*
as a traditional bound book at:
www.1stWorldLibrary.org/purchase.asp?ISBN=1-4218-1560-5

1st World Library Literary Society is a nonprofit
organization dedicated to promoting literacy by:

- Creating a free internet library accessible from any
  computer worldwide.
- Hosting writing competitions and offering book
  publishing scholarships.

Walter Sherwood's Probation
contributed by Tim, Ed & Rodney
in support of
1st World Library Literary Society

CHAPTER I

WALTER SHERWOOD'S LETTER

"Here's a letter for you, Doctor Mack," said the housekeeper, as she entered the plain room used as a library and sitting-room by her employer, Doctor Ezekiel Mack. "It's from Walter, I surmise." This was a favorite word with Miss Nancy Sprague, who, though a housekeeper, prided herself on having been a schoolmistress in her earlier days.

"Indeed, Nancy. Let me see it. Walter is really getting attentive. His last letter came to hand only two days since. He hasn't forgotten his old guardian."

"Oh, no, sir. He'll never do that. He has a predilection for his old home. His heart is in the right place."

"Just so. I wish I felt as sure about his head."

Doctor Mack adjusted his spectacles, for he was rising sixty, and his eyes required assistance, and opened the letter. As he read it his forehead contracted, and he looked disturbed. A perusal of the letter may help us to understand why. It ran as follows:

"DEAR GUARDIAN: You will be surprised at hearing from me so soon again, but I am really forced to write. I find college life much more expensive than I supposed it would be. A fellow is expected to join two or three societies, and each costs money. I know you wouldn't have me appear mean. Then the students have been asked to contribute to a fund for the enlargement of the library, and almost every day there is a demand for money for one object or another. As it is nearly the end of the term, I calculate that with a check for an extra hundred dollars I can get along. I am awfully sorry to ask for it, but it will come out of the money father left me, and I am sure he would wish me to keep up appearances, and not fall behind the rest of the boys.

"I stand fairly well in my studies, and I expect to be stroke oar of the college boat club. Besides this, I have been elected catcher of the college baseball club. I am thought to excel in athletic sports, and really enjoy my college life very much. Please send me the check by return of mail. Affectionately yours, WALTER."

Doctor Mack laid the letter on the table, and slowly removed the glasses from his nose.

"One hundred dollars!" he repeated. "That is the second extra check he has written for, this term. Then his regular term bills will come due in two weeks. He is spending more than three times as much as I did when in college. Forty years have made a difference, no doubt, but not so great a difference as that. I hope the boy isn't falling into extravagant habits. I care for that more than for the money. His father left a good fortune, of which fact he is unfortunately aware, but I don't mean that it shall spoil him. Now, what shall I do.

Horatio Alger, Jr.

Shall I send him the check or not?"

Doctor Mack leaned back in his chair, and thought busily.

He felt anxious about his ward, who had entered college early and was now only seventeen. Walter Sherwood was a boy of excellent talent and popular manners, but he was inclined to be self-indulgent and had a large capacity for "enjoyment." His guardian had fondly hoped that he would lead the class in scholarship, but instead of this he was only doing "fairly well" in his studies. To be sure, he excelled in athletic sports, but, as Doctor Mack reflected, this was not generally considered the chief aim in a college course, except by some of the students themselves.

"I wish I knew just how Walter is making out," thought the doctor. Then, after a pause, he resumed, with a sudden inspiration: "Why shouldn't I know? I'll go over to Euclid to-morrow with out giving Walter any intimation of my visit, and see for myself."

It may be stated here that Walter Sherwood was a member of the sophomore class in Euclid College, situated in the town of the same name. If the reader does not find Euclid in a list of American colleges, it is because for special reasons I have thought it best to conceal the real name of the college, not wishing to bring the Institution into possible disrepute. There are some who might misjudge the college, because it contained some students who made an unprofitable use of their time.

"Nancy," said Doctor Mack at the supper-table, "you may pack a hand- bag for me. I shall start on a journey to-morrow morning."

"Where to, sir, if I may make so bold as to inquire?"

"I think of going to Euclid."

"To see Master Walter?"

"Exactly."

"You haven't heard any bad news, I hope?" said the housekeeper anxiously.

"Oh, no."

"Then he isn't sick?"

"Quite the contrary. He is quite strong and athletic, I should judge, from his letter."

"He will be glad to see you, sir."

"Well, perhaps so. But you know, Nancy, young people don't miss their parents and guardians as much as they are missed at home. They have plenty of excitement and society at college."

"Yes, sir, that's true, but I'm sure Master Walter won't forget his old home. If you have room for some cookies I will put some into the bag. Walter is fond of them."

"No, I think you needn't do It, Nancy, He has a good boarding-house, and no doubt he gets all the cakes he wants. By the way, I want to take the boy by surprise, so don't write and let him know I'm coming."

Horatio Alger, Jr.

"No, sir, I won't."

This was exactly what the housekeeper had intended to do, for she presumed upon her long service in the family to write a few lines occasionally to the boy whom she had known from the age of six.

"Of course I shall be pleased to give him any message from you."

"Thank you, Doctor Mack. Tell him if he catches cold I can send him some camomile. Camomile tea is excellent in such cases. My mother and grandmother used it all their lives."

"You seem to forget that I am a doctor, Nancy. Not that I object to camomile tea - in its place - though I can truly say that I never hankered after it."

"How long will you be gone, doctor?"

"I can't say exactly. You see, Euclid is nearly two hundred miles off. and I don't know whether I can make connections."

"Oh, well, don't hurry! No doubt Walter will want to keep you with him as long as possible."

"I don't feel so sure of that," thought the doctor shrewdly. "Boys are not usually so fond of the society of their guardians, though I don't doubt Walter has a sincere regard for me. He is a warm-hearted boy."

Doctor Mack was no longer in active practice. Three years before he had selected an assistant - a young Doctor Winthrop - in whom his patients had come to feel confidence, so that when he wanted to go away for a few days there was no serious objection. Unlike some elderly practitioners, Doctor Mack did not feel in the least jealous of his young assistant, but was very glad to note his popularity.

"If any one calls for me, Nancy," he said, "say that I am away for a day or two and they can't do better than go to Doctor Winthrop."

"There are some that like you best, sir."

"No doubt, no doubt! They're used to me, you know. There's a good deal in that. Any that please can wait for me, but my advice to them is to go to Doctor Winthrop."

Nancy packed the doctor's hand-bag, putting in a change of linen, a comb and brush, an extra pair of socks and a couple of handkerchiefs. Then, seeing that there was plenty of room, she slipped in a small box of cookies and a little camomile. The doctor discovered them soon after he started on his journey, and with a smile tossed the camomile out of the window, while he gave the cookies to a poor woman who was traveling with a couple of small children in the same car as himself. So that Nancy Sprague's thoughtfulness was not wholly lost, though the intended recipient did not benefit by it.

Doctor Mack had to wait over at a junction for three hours, owing to some irregularities of the trains, and did not reach Euclid till rather a late hour in the afternoon. He went to the Euclid Hotel, and entered his name, E. MACK, Albany, without adding M.D., and substituting Albany for the small village, thirty miles

Horatio Alger, Jr.

away, where he made his home.

"Strategy, doctor, strategy!" he said to himself, "I have come to spy out the land, and must not make myself too conspicuous. I am traveling, as it were, incognito."

CHAPTER II

DR. MACK GETS SOME INFORMATION

The Euclid Hotel was distant about half a mile from the college buildings. It would hardly have paid expenses but for the patronage it received from the parents and friends of the students, who, especially on public occasions, were drawn to visit Euclid, and naturally put up at the hotel. Then the students, tired, perhaps, of the fare at the college commons, dropped in often and ordered a dinner. So, take it all in all, Euclid Hotel benefited largely by the presence of the college. No students, however, were permitted to board there, as it was thought by the college professors that the atmosphere of the hotel would be detrimental to college discipline and the steady habits they desired to inculcate in the young men under their care.

"I wonder," thought Doctor Mack, after supper was over, "whether I had better go round to the college and make an evening call on Walter?"

He was tempted to do so, for he was fond of his young ward and would have enjoyed seeing him. But then he wished, unobserved, to judge for himself whether Walter was making good use of his privileges, and this made it injudicious for him to disclose his presence in the college town.

Horatio Alger, Jr.

He strolled out into the tavern yard, and observed a young man engaged in some light duties.

"Good evening, sir," said the young man, respectfully.

"Good evening, I suppose you are connected with the hotel?"

"Yes, sir; but I would rather be connected with the college."

"Then you have a taste for study?"

"Yes, sir. I began to prepare for college, and had made some progress in Latin and Greek, when my father died, and that put an end to my prospects."

"That was a pity. Has it destroyed your taste for study?"

"No, I spend an hour after I am through work in keeping up my Latin and Greek, but of course I make slow progress."

"Naturally. Now I have no doubt there are many students who do not appreciate their privileges as much as you do."

"I know it, sir. There are pretty lively boys in college. Have you a son there?"

"No."

"I didn't know but what you might have."

"What do you mean by lively?"

"I mean they care more to have a good time than to get on in their studies."

"What do they do?"

"Well, some of them belong to societies, and have a good time whenever they meet. Frequently they give little suppers at the hotel here, and keep it up till a late hour."

"Do the faculty know of this?"

"They may surmise something, but they don't interfere. Of course, it pays Mr. Daniels, the landlord, for he charges a good round sum, and, as there is no other place for the boys to go, they must pay it. There's going to be a supper here to-night."

"Indeed!"

"It is given by one of the sophomores, Walter Sherwood."

"What name did you mention?" asked Doctor Mack, startled.

"Walter Sherwood. Do you know him?"

"I know a family by the name of Sherwood," answered Doctor Mack, evasively. "What sort of a young man is he?"

"I don't call him a young man. He is only seventeen or eighteen - one of the youngest members of the class. He is very popular among his mates - a regular jolly boy he is."

"Does he stand well in his scholarship?"

The young man laughed.

"I don't think he troubles himself much about studies," he replied, "from all I hear; but he is pretty smart, learns easily, and manages to keep up respectably."

Doctor Mack's heart sank within him. Was this the best that could be said about his ward, the son of his old friend?

"Do you think he is dissipated?" he asked, uneasily.

"Not that I ever heard. He is fond of having a good time, and drinks wine at his suppers, but he isn't what you would call intemperate. He would do better work in college if he wasn't so rich."

"So he is rich, then?"

"He must be, for he spends a good deal of money. Pendleton, one of his classmates, told me that he spent more money than any one in the class."

"That is why he needs so many extra checks," thought the guardian soberly.

"I am sorry he doesn't make better use of his privileges," he said aloud.

"Yes, sir, it is a pity. If he didn't care so much for a good time he might stand at the head of his class - so Pendleton thinks."

"If he were a poor boy, now, you think the result

would be different?" asked Doctor Mack, thoughtfully.

"Yes, sir, I have no doubt of it."

"When does the supper commence?"

"At half-past eight o'clock."

"How long will it keep up?"

"Till near midnight. The landlord makes it a point to have them close before twelve. I hope they won't disturb you, sir."

"Are they likely to make much noise?"

"Well, sir, they make speeches, and do a good deal of singing. Then, college songs are naturally noisy."

"Yes, so I hear."

"What is the number of your room?"

"Number nine."

"Why, you are nearly opposite the room where they will have their supper. I am afraid you won't stand much chance of sleeping early."

"Oh, never mind! I shall get an idea of what a college supper is like."

"So you will. If you open the transom over your door you will have the full benefit of all that goes on."

"That will suit me very well," thought Doctor Mack.

"If you would like to be farther away, the landlord would no doubt change your room."

"Oh, no," said the doctor hastily. "It will suit me very well for once to listen to college songs and get an idea of how college boys enjoy themselves."

"A very sensible old gentleman!" thought James Holden. "Some men of his age would make a fuss."

A little before the time when the students were expected to arrive Doctor Mack shut himself up in his room, taking care to open the transom. He had ascertained from the young man, his informant, that supper had been engaged for twelve, and that the price charged per plate was two dollars and a half, all to be paid by Walter Sherwood.

"That makes thirty dollars," he reflected. "No wonder Walter writes for extra checks. I wonderin this thirty dollars is to figure as a contribution to the library?"

From his window he could see the students as they approached the hotel. Finally he caught sight of Walter, with a college friend on each sides with whom he was chatting gaily.

"What a change!" thought Doctor Mack. "It seems only yesterday that Walter started for college, a bashful, unformed boy, full of good resolutions, and determined to distinguish himself in scholarship. Now he has become a gay butterfly. And, what is worse, he has learned to deceive his old guardian, and his chief aim seems to be to have a good time. What can I do to change his course?"

The good doctor's face assumed a thoughtful look.

"I can tell better after what I shall hear to-night," he said to himself.

It was not long before the guests were all assembled and the feast was to begin.

Some one rapped for attention, and then Doctor Mack recognized the voice of his young ward.

"Gentlemen," he said, "I am glad to welcome you to this festal board. After spending ten or a dozen hours in hard study" - laughter and applause - "we find it pleasant to close our books, to relax our learned brows" - more laughter - "and show our appreciation of the good things of life. As Horace, your favorite, says" - I won't insult you by offering to translate his well-known words - *"dulce est desipere in loco.* That is what has brought us here to-night We want to *desipere in loco."*

"So we do! Good for you!" exclaimed one and another.

"I regret," Walter continued, "that all the professors have declined my urgent invitation to be present on this occasion. Professor Griggs" - the professor of mathematics - "said he would not break away from his regular diet of logarithms and radicals." Great laughter. "I have expressly requested Mr. Daniels to provide no logarithms to-night. They don't agree with my constitution."

"Nor with mine!" "Nor with mine!" echoed one and another.

"I shall expect you all, after the banquet, to do something for the general entertainment. I stipulate, however, that none of the company address us in Latin or Greek." - "We won't!" "We won't!" - "Sufficient for the recitation-room is the evil thereof. But I have spoken long enough. There are times when silence is golden, and one of those times is at hand. Brethren, the feast awaits you! Pitch in!"

The speaker took his seat, and then there was a noise of clinking glasses, and knives and forks came to the front. The banquet had begun.

CHAPTER III

A COLLEGE BANQUET

There was a rattling of knives and forks, a clink of glasses, and a buzz of conversation. Doctor Mack was able to hear considerable of it. There were anecdotes of the professors, accounts of narrow escapes from "flunking" in the recitation-room, and remarks by no means complimentary to some of the text-books in use in college. It was evident that the collegians assembled cared more for a good time than for study. Yet these seemed to be the chosen associates of his ward, the doctor reflected.

As the feast proceeded, he grew more sober. He felt that college life, however much it was doing for the faithful students, was only fostering self-indulgence in his ward.

"Something must be done!" reflected Doctor Mack. "Desperate diseases require desperate remedies."

Again the chairman rapped for order, and again Walter's voice was heard.

"Brothers," he said, "the material part of our banquet is ended. We have gratified our appetites with the savory dishes provided by our friend Daniels. We have quaffed the rare Falernian wine, of a vintage unknown to Horace; we have quickened our wits, as I trust, under those favorable conditions, and the time has now come for the feast of reason and the flow of soul. Exhausted as we are by our labors in the classroom" - great laughter - "we have sought refreshment in the way that is most agreeable. It's a way we have at old Euclid! Sing!"

Immediately the assembled company started up the well-known college song:

"It's a way we have at old Euclid,
It's a way we have at old Euclid,
It's a way we have at old Euclid,
To drive dull care away.
It's a way we have at old Euclid,
It's a way we have at old Euclid,
To drive dull care away.

"And we think it is no sin, sir,
To take the Freshmen in, sir,
And ease them of their tin, sir,
To drive dull care away.
It's a way we have at old Euclid,
It's a way we have at old Euclid,
To drive dull care away."

There were other verses, but these will serve as specimens. All joined in the chorus, and Doctor Mack, who remembered his own college life, felt almost tempted to add his voice to those of the young men in the opposite room.

"But, pshaw!" he thought. "What would Walter and his friends think to hear an old graybeard like me taking part in the convivial songs? There is no great harm in singing college songs, if it is accompanied by good work in the recitation-room."

"Brothers," resumed Walter, "we will do our best to drive dull care away. Let us forget, this happy evening, that there are such things as logarithms, and sines, and tangents, and Greek tragedies. To-night our hearts shall be uplifted by sentiment and song. Brother Corbett, you will oblige us with 'Rumsty Ho!'"

A young man with a pleasant voice sang this song, one unfamiliar to the doctor:

"A beggar man laid himself down to sleep,
Rumsty Ho! rumsty Ho!
A beggar man laid himself down to sleep
By the banks of the Mersey, so high and steep,
Rumsty Ho! rumsty Ho!

"Two thieves came walking by that way,
Rumsty Ho! rumsty Ho!
Two thieves came walking by that way,
And they came to the place where the old man lay,
Rumsty Ho! rumsty Ho!

"They stole his wallet and they stole his staff,
Rumsty Ho! rumsty Ho!
They stole his wallet and they stole his staff,
And then broke out in a great horse-laugh,
Rumsty Ho! rumsty Ho!"

There was more of this song, too. Next came "Crambambuli," and then "Cocach-lunk" both of which were familiar to the doctor.

Then Walter said: "Brothers, I have great pleasure in stating that Professor Griggs has concluded to honor our dinner by his learned presence, and has consented to address us. Permit me to introduce Professor Theophilus Griggs."

One of the company had made up as the mathematical professor. In a nasal tone he made a rambling speech, in which he introduced mathematical allusions, and used some of the favorite phrases of the rather dull and prosy instructor, with whom all the students were familiar, some to their sorrow. It seemed to be very amusing to the boys present, as shown by their hearty laughter, but of course Doctor Mack could not appreciate it.

Other songs and other speeches followed. Though for the most part college songs, there were some of a more serious character. Time slipped by, and at length Doctor Mack saw by his watch that it was half-past eleven.

"How long will they keep it up, I wonder?" he asked himself. "I feel drowsy."

He was answered by the chairman.

"Brothers," he said, "time waits for no man. The hour has arrived when, according to agreement, we must wind up our festivities. Hand in hand we will sing 'Auld Lang Syne,' hoping, at some auspicious season after the coming vacation is over, to have another good time. I thank you all for accepting my invitation, and hope you have enjoyed yourselves."

"Three cheers for Sherwood!" cried one of the company.

They were given with a will. Then the parting song was sung, and the students retired to their rooms in one of the college dormitories.

Doctor Mack went thoughtfully to bed.

"It is well I came," he reflected. "Walter has done nothing decidedly wrong as yet, but it is evident he is not improving."

"Well," said James Holdens as he met Doctor Mack the next morning, "did you hear the boys last night?"

"I couldn't very well help it," answered the doctor, smiling. "That young Sherwood seems to be very popular."

"Yes, sir; he is very free with his money."

"In what other way does he spend it?"

"Mr. Daniels keeps half a dozen horses to let to students and others. Sherwood hires a team at least twice a week, and of course it counts up."

"I was not able to spend money in that way when I attended college."

"Then you are a college graduate?" said Holden.

"Yes."

"Did you graduate at Euclid?"

"No; I am a Yale man."

"I congratulate you, sir; I should like to graduate from Yale.

"I hope you may, some time, my young friend. You would derive more benefit, I'll be bound, than those young roysterers of last evening."

"I hope they didn't keep you awake, sir."

"They certainly did as long as they stayed. I should have gone to bed soon afterward, but that I had something on my mind. By the way, don't mention to any of the students that they had an unseen listener."

"No, sir."

Doctor Mack took the first train after breakfast, and returned to his home without seeing his ward.

Nancy Sprague questioned him eagerly.

"And how is Master Walter?" she asked.

"Very well, indeed, Nancy."

"Was he surprised to see you?" "He didn't see me, Nancy."

"He didn't see you!" ejaculated the housekeeper.

"No; the fact was, I went away on a matter of business, and it was not convenient to call on Walter. But I heard him."

"I don't see how you could have been near him without seeing him."

"I shall see him soon, Nancy, and so will you. In two weeks vacation will be here. Examinations are near, and I might have interfered with his studies," the doctor added, with a little innocent evasion.

"To be sure, sir! To be sure! I make no doubt Master Walter is a great scholar."

"I have very strong doubts on that point myself," thought Doctor Mack, but he did not care to express himself thus to Nancy.

"I am so glad the dear boy is coming home soon," murmured the housekeeper. "He has been studying so hard he needs a good long rest. I will make some cookies expressly for him after he comes. I don't believe he gets any at college."

"I wonder what Nancy would say if she could have seen Walter presiding at the supper, and heard the songs?" thought Doctor Mack.

CHAPTER IV

THE DAY AFTER THE FEAST

The same morning, in a comfortably furnished room in Simpson Hall, sat, or rather lounged, Walter Sherwood.

"I feel sleepy this morning, Gates," he said to his chum. "I can't fix my mind on this confounded logic."

"No wonder, Sherwood. You have good reason to be tired after last evening."

"That's so! We had a good time, though. I am sorry you couldn't accept my invitation."

"I couldn't afford it, Sherwood. You know we are very differently situated. You are rich, while I am the oldest son of a country minister, with all I can do to get through college. As it is, I shall be in debt."

"Why not be in debt to me? You never would accept anything from me."

"Yes, I did. I have let you go to the entire expense of furnishing this room, though I have an equal share in it."

"Oh, that's nothing! You pay me in helping me through my lessons when I am behind. If you hadn't read my Horace to me the other day I should have flunked as sure as can be."

"It would be better for you to get your own lesson, Walter." "Well, I suppose it would," answered his roommate, yawning. "I wish you could drive this logic into my head. I suppose I am unusually stupid this morning."

"Suppose we go over it together."

Fifteen minutes later Walter said complacently: "Thanks, old fellow; you have made it as plain as a pikestaff."

"And very likely you will get a higher mark at the recitation than I."

"Well, perhaps so," laughed Walter. "I suppose it is because I have more cheek than you."

"You can do better on slight preparation, certainly. You talk like a professor when you are on your feet."

"You want to be a professor some time, Gates, don't you?"

"Yes," answered his chum, his face flushing, "I should be proud to become a professor in old Euclid."

"It would be awfully slow, I think," returned Walter, stifling a yawn.

"What then, is your ambition?"

"I want to go out among men. I want to take an active part in the world."

"You will have to work harder than you do in college, then."

"I suppose I shall. But I am young, Gates. I am only seventeen."

"And I am nineteen, and look twenty-one."

"All the better! The older you look the better, If you are going to be a college instructor. I would have to wait a long time if I wanted to, even if I were a good deal wiser than I am now. I am so young, in short, that I can afford to have a good time."

"It seems to me that is all you think of, Sherwood."

"Oh, well, I'll reform in time and become a sober old duffer like you," and Walter Sherwood laughed carelessly.

"I hope, at any rate, that you will change your views of life. You know what Longfellow says: 'Life is real! Life is earnest!'"

"Oh, yes, I know that by heart. But it's no use, Gates, you can't make an old man of me before my time. Will it disturb you if I play a tune or two on my violin?"

"Well, to tell the truth, it will. I want to get my Greek lesson, and you had better do the same."

"No, I will read a novel, and you can read over the Greek to me when you have dug it out."

"I will if you wish, but I am afraid I am spoiling you by doing your studying for you."

"Remember, I was out late last night."

"You have something almost every evening, Walter."

"Oh, well, I'll turn over a new leaf next term."

"Why not begin now?"

"If you knew how stupid I feel you wouldn't ask."

Walter stretched himself out on a comfortable lounge, and took up a new novel which he had partially read, while Gates spread the big Greek lexicon on the study-table, and opening his Aristophanes, began slowly and laboriously to translate it into English.

Fifteen minutes passed when a knock was heard at the door.

"Come in!" called out Walter.

He looked up eagerly, hoping the visitor might prove to be one of his jovial comrades of the night before. But he did not look so well pleased when, as the door opened, he caught sight of the pudgy figure and shrewd face of Elijah Daniels, the proprietor of the Euclid Hotel.

"Good morning, Mr. Daniels." he said, rather apprehensively. "So you have found me out."

"No, I have found you in," returned the landlord, with a smile. "I hope I don't intrude upon, your studies, young gentlemen."

"Well, I am taking a little rest from my labors," said Walter.

"You were up rather late last evening, Mr. Sherwood."

"That's a fact, and you gave us a first-class supper, Daniels. You did yourself proud."

"I did my best, Mr. Sherwood, and I am glad you were satisfied."

"All the fellows praised the supper." "That's good. I know what you young gentlemen like, and I get it, no matter what it costs. I don't make much on the suppers I give the college boys, but of course I like to please them."

"Your price is quite reasonable, I think."

"I am glad you do. I have brought in the bill for last night's entertainment, and if you can let me have the money, I shall be glad."

"Well, the fact is, Daniels, I haven't got the money by me this morning."

The landlord's countenance changed.

"I like prompt pay," he said. "It is a good deal of trouble, and, as I said, there isn't much money to be made."

"That's all right. You won't have to wait long."

"How long, Mr. Sherwood?"

"I expect a check for a hundred dollars from my guardian to-day. I wrote three days since, for I knew you wouldn't like to wait."

"A hundred dollars!" repeated the landlord, feeling a little easier in mind.

"Yes."

"Perhaps your guardian may object to sending it."

"Oh, no! He's a nice old fellow, Doctor Mack is. He is very indulgent."

"What name did you mention?

"Doctor Mack. Ezekiel Mack."

"Indeed! Why, we had a gentleman stopping at the hotel last night of that name."

"What!" ejaculated Walter, in astonishment. "Do you mean to tell me that Doctor Mack - my guardian - was at the hotel last night? It can't be. He would have called on me."

"It may not have been the same man. Now I come to think of it, he didn't put himself down on the book Doctor Mack. He just put himself down E. Mack. He seemed a plain sort of man."

"Where did he register from?" asked Walter eagerly.

"From Albany."

"Is he at the hotel now?"

"He went away by the morning train."

"Then it couldn't have been he," said Walter, in a tone of relief. "He doesn't live in Albany. Besides, he would have called on me. No, it must have been some other Mack."

"Perhaps you wouldn't have liked to have him catch you at a gay supper, Mr. Sherwood?" said the landlord shrewdly.

"Well, no, I'd a little rather receive him in my room, with a book open before me."

"He might object to pay out money for such doings."

"He won't know anything about it. Just leave your bill, Mr. Daniels, and as soon as I get the check I'll call round and pay it."

"There's another bill, too, a livery bill. I brought that along, too."

"How much is it?" asked Walter anxiously.

"Eighteen dollars."

"I didn't think it was as much as that!"

"Bills mount up faster than you young gentlemen think for. I suppose, however, you can afford to pay it?"

"Oh, yes!" said Walter carelessly.

"Your uncle may think it rather steep, eh?"

"I wrote him that I had some extra expenses this time."

"Then I suppose you can't do anything for me this morning?"

"No, Daniels; just leave both bills, and I feel quite sure that I can pay you in a day or two. I suppose you can change a check?"

"I'll manage to."

The landlord retired, leaving the bills behind him.

"Do you know, Sherwood," said his chum gravely "I think you are foolishly extravagant."

"Well, perhaps I am."

"You are spending three times as much as I am."

"I'll do better next term. I wish my guardian would hurry along that check."

Two days later a letter came for Walter in the familiar handwriting of Doctor Mack. He tore it open hastily, and as he read it he turned pale and sank into a chair.

"What's the matter?" asked Gates.

"Matter enough!" answered Walter, in a hollow voice. "My money is lost, and I've got to leave college!"

CHAPTER V

WALTER TAKES MATTERS PHILOSOPHICALLY

Walter's announcement, recorded at the close of the preceding chapter, fell like a thunderbolt on his roommate.

"You have lost your money?" repeated Gates, in a tone of incredulity. "You don't mean it!"

"Read that letter, Gates," said Walter, pushing it over to his chum.

The letter was, of course, from Doctor Mack, and ran thus:

"DEAR WALTER: Your letter asking for an extra check for one hundred dollars came to hand three or four days since. I have delayed answering for two reasons. I am satisfied that you are spending more money than is necessary, and, moreover, I have shrunk from communicating to you some unpleasant intelligence. Upon me have devolved the investment and management of your property, and while I have tried to be cautious, there have been losses which I regret. In one case three-fourths of an investment has been lost. Of course, you didn't know this, or you would have been less free in your expenditures.

"I am not prepared to tell you how you stand. I think it will be prudent for you to leave college at the end of this term, and for a year to seek some employment. During that time I will do what I can to settle matters on a better footing, and perhaps at the end of that time you will be able to return to your studies. You are so young - I think you must be younger than the majority of your classmates - that you can afford to lose the time.

"I send you a check for sixty dollars in place of a hundred. I wish you to have your regular term bills sent to me, and I will forward checks in payment. I will see that you leave Euclid owing no man anything. When you come home for the vacation we can consult as to the future. I hope you will not be much depressed or cast down by the news I send. Your money is not all lost, and I may be able, in the course of twelve months, to recover in a large measure what has been sunk.

"Your affectionate guardian,

EZEKIEL MACK."

"A regular sockdolager, isn't it, Gates?" said Walter.

"I don't see that it's so bad," answered Gates slowly. "Your money isn't all lost."

"But I must leave college."

"True; but, as your guardian says, you are young, and if you come back at the end of a year you will still be a year younger than I for your standing. Of course, I am sorry to have you go."

"I am sure of that, Gates."

"Is the prospect of working for a year so unpleasant to you, Walter?"

"No, I can't say it is," said Walter, brightening up, "not if I can choose my employment. I shouldn't like to go behind the counter in a grocery store, or -"

"Black boots for a living?"

"Well, hardly," said Walter, laughing.

"Probably your guardian will consult your preferences."

"I wish I could arrange to travel. I should like to see something of the world."

"Why not? You might get an agency of some kind. One college vacation - last summer - I traveled about as book agent."

"How did you like it?"

"Not very much. I met with a good many rebuffs, and was occasionally looked upon with suspicion, as I could see. Still, I made a living, and brought back thirty dollars to start me on my new term."

"Just what my supper cost the other evening."

"Yes; I didn't think it wise to spend the money in the

same way."

"You have cheered me up, Gates. I really believe I shall like to spend a year in some kind of business."

"Write your guardian to that effect. He may be blaming himself for his agency in your misfortune, and a cheerful letter from you will brighten him up."

"All right! I will."

Walter sat down and dashed off the following note:

"DEAR GUARDIAN: Your letter just received. I won't pretend that I am not sorry for the loss of my money, but I am sure that you acted for the best. Don't trouble yourself too much about the matter. Perhaps it will all come out right in a year or so. In the meantime I think I shall find it not unpleasant to work for a year if you will let me select the kind of business I am to follow.

"I will make the money you sent me do for the present, and will send you my term bills as you desire. You can depend upon my settling up as cheap as possible, though I confess I have not hitherto been nearly as economical as I might have been. Now that I know it is necessary, you shall have no reason to complain of me.

"Your affectionate ward,

WALTER SHERWOOD."

"What do you think of that, Gates?" asked Walter, giving the letter to his chum to read.

"Excellent! It shows the right spirit."

"I am glad you think so."

"Do you know, Walter, I think I have more occasion for regret than you? I must bid farewell to my room-mate and this pleasant room."

"To your room-mate, yes, but not necessarily to the room."

"I shall have to furnish it in very different style for the present. I am not sure that I can afford a carpet. The luxury of my present surroundings, I am afraid, will spoil me for humble quarters."

"Don't borrow any trouble about that. I shall leave you the furniture as it stands, and when I come back to college, even if we are in different classes, you must take me in again."

"Of course I will agree to an arrangement so much in my favor, but perhaps your guardian will think you had better sell the furniture and realize what you can."

"No, I am sure he won't. There's nothing mean about Doctor Mack. You can take in any one you please in my place, only I am to come back at the end of a year if things turn out well."

"I heartily hope you will come back, and if you will excuse my saying so, with a more earnest spirit, and a determination to do justice to your really excellent talents."

"Good advice! I'll adopt it. I'll begin to do better at

once. I was intending to take a drive this evening, but it would cost me two dollars, and I will stay at home and save the money."

"Come with me on a walk, instead."

"I will."

"We will go to the top of Mount Legar. At sunset there will be a fine view from there."

"I must stop on the way and pay Mr. Daniels what I owe him. He will lose a good deal by my going away."

"True; but his loss will be your gain."

At the outset of their walk the two students called at the hotel, and found Mr. Daniels on the piazza.

"Glad to see you, Mr. Sherwood," said the landlord briskly.

"I think you will be, Mr. Daniels, for I have come to pay your bills."

"Money is always welcome, Mr. Sherwood. You have no idea how much I lose by trusting students. There was Green, of the last graduating class, left college owing me forty-five dollars. He has gone West somewhere, and I never expect to get a cent of my money."

"You came pretty near losing by me, Daniels."

"How is that?" queried the landlord, looking surprised.

"I've lost a lot of money, or my guardian has for me,

and I've got to leave college at the end of this term."

"You don't say so!" ejaculated Mr. Daniels regretfully.

"It's all true. My guardian wrote me about it this morning."

"I suppose you're a good deal cut up about it, Mr. Sherwood."

"Well, I was at first, but I may be able to come back after a year or two. I shall go into some business, and meanwhile my guardian will do what he can to recover the money lost. It isn't so bad, after all."

"I shall be sorry to have you go, Mr. Sherwood."

"You will miss my bills, at any rate. I wouldn't have given that supper the other evening if I had known how things stood. I would have put the thirty dollars to better use."

"Well, you've paid up like a gentleman, anyway. I hope you'll come back in a year as rich as ever. You wanted a team to-night, James told me."

"That was before I got my guardian's letter. I shall walk, instead of taking a carriage-ride."

"I will let the account stand, if you wish."

"No. I can't afford to run up any bills. Good night, Mr. Daniels."

"You did right, Walter," said Gates. "It is a bad thing to run up bills."

"Especially when you are poor. It seems odd to be poor."

"I am used to it, Walter. You don't seem very sad over it."

"I am not. That is what puzzles me. I really begin to think I like it."

Horatio Alger, Jr.

CHAPTER VI

TRUE FRIEND AND FALSE

A college community is for the most part democratic. A poor student with talent is quite as likely to be a favorite as the heir to a fortune, often more so. But there are always some snobs who care more for dollars than sense. So Walter was destined to find out, for he made no secret of his loss of fortune. Most of his college friends sympathized with him, but there was one who proved unreliable.

This was Harvey Warner, the son of a man who had made a fortune during the Civil War, some said as a sutler. Harvey professed to be very aristocratic, and had paid especial attention to Walter, because he, too, had the reputation of being wealthy. He had invited Walter to pass a couple of weeks at the summer residence of the Warners, near Lake George. This, however, was before he had heard of Walter's loss of fortune. As soon as be learned this, he decided that the invitation must be withdrawn. This would be awkward, as he had been on very intimate terms with our hero, and had been a guest at the banquet.

Not foreseeing the effect of his changed circumstances on the mind of his late friend, Walter, meeting him on the campus the day afterward, called out, familiarly:

"How are you, old fellow? Why didn't you come round to my room last evening?"

"I had another engagement, Sherwood," answered Warner, stiffly.

"You ought to give me the preference," said Walter, not observing the other's change of manner.

"Ahem! a man must judge for himself, you know. By the way, is it true that you have lost all your money?"

"I don't know how much I have lost, but I am not coming back to college next year."

"You are in hard luck," said Warner coldly. "By the way, I think we shall have to give up that plan for the summer."

"What plan?"

"Why, you know I invited you to visit me at Lake George."

Walter began to comprehend.

"Why, are you not going to be there?" he asked,

"Yes, but the house will be full of other fellows, don't you know."

"So that there will be no room for me," said Walter calmly, looking Warner full in the face.

"Awfully sorry, and all that sort of thing," drawled

Warner. "Besides, I suppose you will have to go to work."

"Yes, I expect to go to work - after awhile. Probably I shall take a few weeks for rest. By the way, when did you find out that your home would be full - of other fellows?"

"Got a letter from my sister this morning. Besides - in your changed circumstances, don't you know, you might find it awkward to be living in a style you couldn't keep up."

"Thank you, Warner. You are very considerate. I really didn't give you credit for so much consideration."

"Don't mention it! Of course with your good sense you understand?"

"I think I do."

"And, by the way, I believe you borrowed two dollars of me last week. If it is inconvenient for you to pay the whole at once, you might hand me a dollar."

"And I called that fellow my friend!" said Walter to himself.

"You are very considerate again, but I think I would rather pay the whole at once. Can you change a ten?"

Harvey Warner looked surprised. He had jumped to the conclusion that Walter was the next thing to a pauper, and here he was better supplied with money than himself.

"I am not sure that I have as much money here," he said.

"Then come with me to the drug-store; I am going to buy a bottle of tooth-wash, and will change the bill there."

Warner accepted this proposal.

"I'd better make sure of my money while he has it," he reflected.

"I hope you're not very much disappointed about the visit?" he said.

"Not at all! I should have had to decline. I have been invited to spend a month at the Adirondacks with Frank Clifford."

"You don't mean it!" ejaculated Warner enviously.

Clifford was a member of an old family, and an invitation from him was felt to confer distinction. Warner himself would have given a good deal to be on sufficiently intimate terms to receive such a compliment.

"When did he invite you?" he asked suggestively.

Walter saw what was in his mind, and answered, with a smile:

"He invited me this morning."

"Had he heard -"

"Of my loss of fortune? Oh, yes! But why should that make any difference?"

"I wouldn't go, if I were you."

"Why not?"

"You are going to be a poor man."

"I don't know about that."

"You are poor now, at any rate."

"Well, perhaps so, but am I any the worse for that?"

"I thought you would understand my meaning."

"I do, but I am glad that all my friends don't attach the importance you do to the possession of fortune. Good morning!"

"I suppose it's the way of the world!" thought Walter, as his quondam friend left him. "But, thank Heaven, all are not mercenary! I've got a few friends left, anyhow."

A few rods farther on he met Victor Creswell, perhaps the richest student in the junior class.

"What's this I hear, Walter?" he asked. "Have you lost your money?"

"Some of it, I believe."

"And you are not coming back to college?"

"I shall stay out a year. Perhaps I can come back then."

"You needn't leave at all. My governor allows me a hundred dollars a month for my own use - spending money, you know. I'll give you half of it, if that will enable you to pull through."

Walter was touched.

"You are a friend worth having, Creswell," he said. "But I really think I shall enjoy being out of college for a year. I shall find out what is in me. But I sha'n't forget your generous offer."

"Better accept it, Sherwood. I can get along well enough on fifty dollars a month."

"I won't accept it for myself, but I'll tell you something. My chum, Gates, is very hard pushed. You know he depends wholly on himself, and twenty-five dollars just at this time would be a godsend to him. He is worried about paying his bills. If, now, you would transfer a little at your generosity to him - "

"I don't know him very well, but if you speak well of him that is enough. I shall be glad to help him. Let me see how much I can spare."

He drew out a wallet, and from it four ten dollar bills.

"Here are forty dollars," he said. "Give them to him, but don't let him know where they came from." "Creswell, you're a trump!" said Walter, shaking his hand vigorously. "You don't know how happy you will make him."

"Oh, that's all right. But I'm sorry you won't let me do something for you."

"I will if I need it."

"Good!" said Creswell, in a tone of satisfaction. "Now, mind, you don't hesitate."

Walter, happy in the happiness he was going to confer, made his way quickly to his own room. Gates sat at the table with a troubled brow, writing some figures on a piece of paper.

"What are you about, Gates?" asked his chum.

"I have been thinking." said Gates wearily, "that perhaps I ought to do what you have decided to do."

"What's that?"

"Leave college.

"But why?"

"I am so troubled to pay my bills. I wrote to my uncle last week - he is a well-to-do farmer - asking him if he wouldn't send me fifteen dollars to help pay my term bills. I promised to come and help him in the farm work during July."

"What does he say?" asked Walter, smiling, Gates couldn't understand why.

"That he never pays for work in advance - he doesn't approve of it."

"He could afford it?"

"Oh, yes; he's got a good sum in the savings-bank, but

he is a very cautious man. I don't see how I'm going to get through. Perhaps I had better take a year away from college."

"There is no need of that. I have some money here for you."

"Some money for me?"

"Yes," and Walter placed four ten-dollar bills on the table.

"But, Walter, you are in no position to lend me money."

"True; the money doesn't come from me."

"But who besides you would do me such a great favor?"

"One of the rich fellows in college - no, I can't tell you his name. You can take it without hesitation."

"But it must have been to you that he lent it."

"No, he understands that it is to be given to you. Will it help you?"

"Will it help me? It will carry me through gloriously," and Gates was radiant with pleasure.

"Are you going to leave college now?"

"No; this help is providential. I will never be distrustful again."

"I wish Creswell could see how much happiness his gift has brought with it," thought Walter.

CHAPTER VII

WALTER'S EXPERIMENT BEGINS

After a conference between Walter and his guardian it was decided that he should wait till the first of September before seeking for any business position. Walter, who was somewhat impulsive, was disposed to start at once, but Doctor Mack said: "No, you are entitled to a vacation. When your class resumes study at Euclid, it will be time for you to begin to earn your living."

"I am not sure that I deserve a vacation," said Walter frankly. "I have not studied as hard at I ought."

"Very probably. You have not been in earnest. You are a year older now, and you have a better understanding of your position."

"You are very charitable, my dear guardian," said Walter.

Doctor Mack smiled.

"I am quite aware," he said, "that old heads are not often to be found on young shoulders."

"Then you think it will be right for me to enjoy myself

this summer?"

"I want you to do so."

"One of my college friends, Frank Clifford, has invited me to pass a month with him in the Adirondacks. The Cliffords have a lodge not far from Blue Mountain Lake. Frank's mother and sisters will be abroad, and he wants me to keep him company."

"I can think of no objection. How shall you spend your time?"

"In hunting and fishing. There are splendid chances for both up there, so Clifford says."

"Go and have your good time. When you come back we will talk of your future plans."

Walter's stay was prolonged to eight weeks, and when he returned it was already nearing the end of August. He was browned by exposure, and looked the picture of health.

"Now I am ready to go to work, Doctor Mack," he said. "Have you any plans for me?"

"How would you like to go into a drug-store? I have a college classmate who is a very successful druggist in Syracuse."

Walter shrugged his shoulders.

"I don't believe I have a taste for making pills," he said.

"I thought not. What do you think of entering a dry-goods store? I am acquainted with the head of a prominent establishment in New York."

"It is a very respectable position, but I should feel cabined, cribbed, confined in it."

"I am at the end of my tether. Have you formed any plans of your own?"

"Well, not exactly."

"But you have thought somewhat on the subject?"

"Yes," answered Walter.

"If at all possible, I shall let you have your own way."

"You may think me foolish," said Walter hesitatingly.

"I don't know. Let me hear what you have to propose."

"I thought," said Walter eagerly, "I would like to go out West."

"What would you do when you got there?"

"There must be lots of things to do."

"Very likely. You might buy an ax and clear the virgin forests."

"I am afraid I wouldn't be a success at that."

"You have no definite idea as to what you would do?"

"No. I could tell better when I got out there."

"Now, about the expense. How much money would you need? You would require to live till you begin to earn something."

"How much will it cost me to get to Chicago?"

"Say about twenty-five dollars."

"I think, guardian, if you will advance me a hundred dollars, that will be sufficient."

"For how long a time?"

"For a year. You see, I expect to earn my own living by the time I have spent fifty dollars in all. I should go to a cheap boarding-place, of course. I should be able to pay my way."

"You will be content, then, with a hundred dollars, Walter?"

"Yes; perhaps I could make it do on less."

"No; you shall have a hundred. If absolutely necessary, you can send for more."

"No," said Walter confidently; "I won't do that. I shall get along somehow. I want to make a man of myself."

"That is a commendable ambition. Still, sometimes a young man finds it hard to obtain employment. If you had a trade, now, it might be different. Suppose, for instance, you were a journeyman tailor, you could readily find a place in Chicago or any good-sized city."

"I shouldn't care to be a tailor."

"I shouldn't care to employ you if you were," said his guardian, smiling. "One thing I would like to guard you against. Don't be too particular about what you take up. With so small an outfit as you have stipulated for, you will have to go to work at something soon. Then, again, you won't be able to live as well as you have been accustomed to do here and in college."

"I understand that, and am prepared for it. I want to rough it."

"Possibly you will have your wish granted. I don't want to discourage you, Walter. I only want to prepare you for what may, and probably will, come."

"Do you know any one in Chicago, Doctor Mack? I might find it pleasant to have an acquaintance."

"Yes, I know a retired merchant named Archer. He lives on Indiana Avenue. I don't remember the number, but you can easily find his name in the directory. His name is Allen Archer."

Walter noted the name in a new memorandum book which he had purchased.

"Where would you advise me to put up on my arrival in Chicago?" he asked.

"There are several good houses - the Sherman, Tremont, Palmer House; but they will be beyond your means. Indeed, any hotel will be. Still you might go to some good house for a day. That will give you time to hunt up a modest boarding-house."

"An excellent plan!" said Walter, in a tone of

satisfaction. "Do you know, my dear guardian, I shall go out in the best of spirits. I feel - in Shakespeare's words - that the world is mine oyster."

"I hope you will be able to open it, Walter. You have my best wishes. Don't forget that you will have to depend on yourself."

"I won't forget it. I wish it was time for me to start."

"It will come soon enough. You had better get out your clothes, and get them mended, if necessary, and put in order. Nancy will do all she can for you, and the tailor will do the rest. Better not take much with you. When you get settled I will forward your trunk by express."

When Nancy Sprague heard of Walter's plans she was much disturbed.

"Oh, Master Walter," she said, in a tragic tone, "is it true that you've lost all your money and have got to go out into the cold world to make a living?"

"I believe I have lost some money, Nancy, but I rather like the idea of working for my living."

"Oh, you poor child, you little know what it is. I can't bear to think of it. I can't see how Doctor Mack can let you go."

"I should be very sorry if he refused. It isn't so bad, to work for a living. Haven't you always done it?"

"Yes, but that's different. I was always poor, and I am used to it."

"I'm going to get used to it."

"Walter - don't tell your guardian what I am saying - but I've got two hundred dollars in the savings bank, and I shall be very glad to give you some of it. You will take it, now, won't you? I can get it out to-morrow."

"Nancy, you are a true friend," said Walter, really moved by the unselfish devotion of the house-keeper; "but I sha'n't need it. I shall take a hundred dollars with me, and long before it is gone I shall be earning my living."

"You'll send for it if you need it?"

"Yes; if I find I am very hard up, and there is no other way, I will send for it."

Nancy brightened up, much pleased and relieved by this assurance.

"I couldn't bear to think of your suffering for a meal of victuals when we have so much in the house. I don't see why you can't stay at home and get a place in the village."

Walter laughed.

"It wouldn't suit me at all, Nancy. I am going West to grow up with the country."

"I wish I could be somewhere near, to look after you."

"It would be of no use, Nancy. Women are in great demand out there - at any rate in Dakota - and you'd be married in less than no time, if you went."

"You are only joking now, Master Walter."

"Not at all! I read the other day that of ten school-ma'ams who went out to Dakota last fall, eight were married within three months."

"Nobody could marry me against my will," said Nancy resolutely.

"Perhaps he would find a way of overcoming your objections," said Walter, laughing. "But I am afraid Doctor Mack couldn't do without you. He couldn't spare you and me both."

"That's true," assented Nancy, who had not been so much alarmed at the matrimonial dangers hinted at by Walter as might have been anticipated. Had a good opportunity offered, I am inclined to think Nancy would have been willing to change her name. After all, she was only forty-nine, and I have known more than one to surrender single blessedness with all its charms at and beyond that age.

At last the day of departure came. Valise in hand, Walter jumped aboard the stage that was to convey him to the railroad-station. He shook hands with his guardian and Nancy, the driver whipped up his horses, and a new period in Walter's life had commenced.

"I wonder how he'll come out?" mused Doctor Mack thoughtfully. "Have I acted for the best in letting him go? Well, time alone can tell."

CHAPTER VIII

WALTER BUYS A WATCH

Walter was tempted to stop over at Niagara, as his ticket would have allowed him to do, but he was also very anxious to reach Chicago and get to work. "I can visit Niagara some other time," he reflected. "Now I can spare neither the money nor the time."

Hour after hour sped by, until with a little thrill of excitement Walter learned by consulting his railroad guide that he was within fifty miles of Chicago. He looked out of the car window, and surveyed with interest the country through which they were speeding at the rate of thirty-five miles an hour. His attention was drawn from the panorama outside by a voice:

"Is this seat engaged?"

Walter looked up, and his glance rested on a man of perhaps thirty-five, dressed in a light suit, and wearing a tall white hat.

"No, sir," answered Walter politely, removing his gripsack from the seat.

"I don't want to incommode you," said the stranger, as he took the place thus vacated.

"You don't in the least," said Walter.

"I suppose you are going to Chicago?"

"Yes, sir."

"Are you going farther - out to Dakota, for instance?"

"No, sir. Chicago is far enough west for me at present."

"I live in Dakota. I have a long journey to make after we reach Chicago." "I don't know about Dakota. Is it a good place for business?"

"It is going to be. Yes, Dakota has a bright future. I have a pleasant little home out there. I had to go East on business, and stayed a little longer than I intended. In fact I spent more money than I anticipated, and that makes me a little short."

It struck Walter that his new acquaintance for a stranger was very confidential.

"Is it possible he will propose to borrow money of me?" he asked himself. He did not quite know what to say, but politeness required him to say something.

"I am sorry," he replied, in a sympathizing tone.

"I should like to take a train this evening for my home," continued the stranger.

"I hope you will be able to do so."

"Well, there's one drawback. I haven't got money enough to buy a through ticket. Under these circumstances I am going to offer you a bargain."

Walter looked surprised and expectant. The stranger drew a gold watch from his pocket - a very handsome gold watch, which looked valuable.

"You see that watch?" he said. "How much do you think it is worth?"

"It looks like a nice watch. I am no judge of values."

"It cost me ninety dollars six months since. Now I need the money, and I will sell it to you for twenty-five."

"But that would be a great sacrifice."

"So it would, but I need the money. Of course, if you haven't got the money -"

"I have that amount of money," said Walter, "but I haven't got it to spare. I might need it."

"Then all you need to do is to sell the watch or pawn it. You could sell it for fifty dollars without trouble."

"Why don't you do that?" asked Walter shrewdly.

"Because I haven't the time. I want, if possible, to go on to-night. If you had a wife and two children waiting for you, whom you had not seen for two months, you wouldn't mind losing a few dollars for the sake of seeing them a little sooner."

"Very likely," answered Walter, to whom his companion's explanation seemed plausible.

Walter was tempted, but he reflected that twenty-five dollars represented a third of the money he had with him, so he put away the temptation, but with reluctance. He had a silver watch, bought for him, when he entered college, at a cost of fifteen dollars, and like the majority of boys of his age he felt that he should much prefer to carry a gold one. Still he must be prudent.

"No," he said, shaking his head, "I don't think I had better buy the watch. I presume you will find some one else on the train who would be glad of the bargain."

"Very likely, but we are near Chicago, and I haven't time to look around. Come, I'll make you a still better offer, though I ought not to do so. You may have the watch for twenty dollars. That money will get me through, and I won't haggle about five dollars."

"Twenty dollars!" repeated Walter thoughtfully.

"Yes, look at the watch. Isn't it a beauty?"

"Yes; I like the appearance of it very much."

"If you get out of money, you can easily pawn it for more than the sum I ask for it."

Certainly this was an important consideration. Walter felt that he would be foolish to lose so good a chance. It was a pity that the stranger should be forced to make such a sacrifice, yet it really seemed that he would be doing him a favor, as well as benefiting himself, by accepting his proposition.

"You will guarantee it to be solid gold?" he said, with

momentary suspicion.

"Certainly. You will see that it is an Elgin watch. Of course you know the reputation of that make. They don't make any sham watches at their factory."

"I thought the case might be gilt," said Walter, half ashamed of his suspicions.

"You do well to be cautious, but I will guarantee the watch to be all I represent it. I only wish you were a jeweler. Then you could judge for yourself."

It sounded very plausible. Then, the watch was a very handsome one.

"Let me open it and show you the works."

The stranger did so. Walter was no judge of the mechanism of a watch, but what he saw impressed him favorably. The stranger seemed very frank and fair-spoken. Walter knew, of course, that in traveling one was likely to meet with sharpers, but that did not justify him in suspecting everybody he met.

"It would look very nice at the end of my chain," he thought. "I suppose I cannot afford it; but, as he says, I can raise money on it at any time."

"Well, young man, what is your decision? You must excuse me for hurrying, but we are not far from Chicago, and I want to make sure that I can continue my journey to-night. I shall telegraph to my wife that I am coming."

"I will take the watch," said Walter. "There doesn't

seem to be much risk in doing so."

"Bosh! I should say not. Young man, I congratulate you. You have made the best bargain of your life. Have you got the money handy?"

Walter took out two ten-dollar bills and handed them to his companion, receiving the watch in exchange.

"Well, that settles my mind," said the stranger, in a tone of satisfaction. "I shall see the old woman and the kids very soon, thanks to your kindness."

"Don't mention it," said Walter complacently. "I feel indebted to you, rather, as you have given me much more than an equivalent for my money."

"That is true, but under present circumstances money is worth a good deal to me. Now, if you don't mind I will go into the smoking-car and have a little smoke before we arrive. Will you join me?"

"No, sir, thank you; I don't smoke."

"Good-day, then. Hope we shall meet again."

Walter responded politely, and the stranger, rising, walked forward to the front part of the car and disappeared.

Walter detached the silver watch from the plated chain to which it was attached, substituted the new gold watch, and put the silver watch in his pocket. It occurred to him that if he should really need money it might be better for him to sell the silver watch and retain the gold one.

"I have made thirty dollars at the very least on my purchase," he reflected, "for I am sure I can sell the watch for fifty dollars if I wish to do so. This is a white day for me, as the Romans used to say. I accept it as a good omen of success. I wish Doctor Mack and Nancy were here to see it. I think the doctor would give me credit for a little shrewdness."

The car sped on perhaps a dozen miles farther, when the door opened and the conductor entered, followed by a stout man of perhaps fifty years of age, who looked flushed and excited.

"This gentleman has been robbed of his gold watch," explained the conductor. "He is convinced that some one on the train has taken it. Of course, no one of you is suspected, but I will trouble you to show me your watches."

As Walter heard these words a terrible fear assailed him. Had he bought a stolen watch?

CHAPTER IX

AN INGENIOUS SCHEME

The passengers, though somewhat surprised, generally showed their watches with a good grace. One old man produced a silver watch fifty years old.

"That watch belonged to my grandfather," he said. "You don't claim that, do you?"

"Wouldn't take it as a gift," said the loser crustily.

"You couldn't get it in exchange for yours!" retorted the owner.

Presently they came to Walter. If he had not attached the gold watch to his chain, instead of his old silver one, he would have been tempted to leave it in his pocket and produce the less valuable one. But he was saved from the temptation, as this would now have been impossible. Besides, had the gold watch been found on him afterward it would have looked very suspicious.

"Well, youngster," said the stout man, "show us your watch."

With a flushed face and an uneasy feeling Walter drew

out the gold timepiece.

"Is that your watch?" he said.

"Yes!" almost shouted the stout passenger, fiercely. "So you are the thief?"

"No, sir," answered Walter, pale but firm. "I am not the thief."

"Where did you get it, then?"

"I bought it."

"You bought it? That's a likely story. "Why, it was taken from me this very afternoon."

"That may be, but I bought it, all the same."

The owner was about to protest, when the conductor said quietly: "Listen to the young fellow's explanation."

Walter proceeded:

"A man came to my seat and told me he wanted to raise enough money to get to Dakota. He offered me the watch for twenty-five dollars, though he said it cost him ninety six months ago."

"And you paid him twenty-five dollars?"

"No; I had no money to spare, but when he offered it for twenty, and told me I could more than get my money back either by pawning or selling it, I made up my mind to purchase, and did so."

"Where is this man?" asked the conductor.

"He said he was going into the smoking-car."

"That's a likely story," sneered the stout gentleman.

"Do you charge me with taking the watch?" demanded Walter hotly. "I have never left this car. Have you seen me before?"

"No; but you are probably a confederate of the man from whom you got it. But I am not sure if there was any such man."

"I will describe him," said Walter.

As he did so, the conductor said: "There was such a man on the train. He got off at the last station."

"I don't know anything about that," said the claimant; "but I'll trouble you, young man, for that watch."

"Will you return me the twenty dollars I gave for it?" asked Walter.

"Of course not. I don't propose to buy back my own watch."

An elderly gentleman who sat just behind Walter spoke up here.

"It is rather hard on the boy," he said. "I can confirm his story about the purchase of the watch. I heard the bargaining and saw the purchase-money paid."

"That makes no difference to me," said the claimant.

"I've identified the watch and I want it."

Walter removed it from his chain and was about to hand it to the claimant, when a quiet-looking man, dressed in a drab suit, rose from a seat farther down the car and came forward. He was a small man, not over five feet five inches in height, and he would not have weighed over one hundred and twenty pounds, but there was a look of authority on his face and an accent of command in his voice.

"You needn't give up the watch, my boy," he said.

Walter drew back his hand and turned round in surprise. The claimant uttered an angry exclamation, and said testily: "By what right do you interfere?"

"The watch isn't yours," said the small man nonchalantly.

"It isn't, hey? Well, of all the impertinent -"

"Stop there, Jim Beckwith! You see I know you" - as the stout man turned pale and clutched at the side of the seat.

"Who are you?" he demanded hoarsely.

"Detective Green!"

The claimant lost all his braggadocio air, and stared at the detective with a terrified look.

"That isn't my name," he managed to ejaculate.

"Very likely not," said the detective calmly, "but it is

one of your names. It is a very clever game that you and your confederate are playing. He sells the watch, and you demand it, claiming that it has been stolen from you. I was present when the watch was sold, and the reason I did not interfere was because I was waiting for the sequel. How many times have you played this game?"

"There's some mistake," gasped the other.

"Perhaps so, but I have some doubts whether you came by it honestly."

"I assure you it is my watch," cried the other, uneasily.

"How much did you pay for it, young man?" asked the detective.

"Twenty dollars."

"Very well, sir; give the boy twenty dollars, and I shall advise him to give the watch back to you, as it may be stolen property, which he would not like to have found in his possession."

"But that will be paying twenty dollars for my own property. It was not to me he paid the money."

"You will have to look to your confederate for that. I am not sure but I ought to make you give twenty-five dollars."

This hint led to the stout man's hastily producing two ten-dollar bills, which he tendered to Walter.

"It's an outrage," he said, "making a man pay for his

own property!"

"Are you sure that your statements in regard to this man are true?" asked an important-looking individual on the opposite side of the car. "To my mind your interference is unwarrantable, not to say outrageous. Justice has been trampled upon."

The detective looked round sharply.

"Do you know the man?" he asked.

"No."

"Well, I do. I first made his acquaintance at Joliet prison, where he served a term of years for robbing a bank. Is that true or not, Jim Beckwith?"

The man known as Beckwith had already started to leave the car, but, although he heard the question, he didn't come back to answer it.

"I generally know what I'm about," continued the detective, pointedly, "as those who are unwise enough to criticise my actions find out, sooner or later."

The important gentleman did not reply, but covered his confusion by appearing to be absorbed in a daily paper, which he held up before his face.

"You let him off easy," said the gentleman in the rear seat. "You allowed him to take the watch. I was surprised at that."

"Yes; for, strange as it may seem, it was probably his, though the money with which he bought it may have

Horatio Alger, Jr.

been stolen. That watch has been probably sold a dozen times and recovered the same way. Were it a stolen watch, the risk would be too great. As it is I had no pretext for arresting him."

"Was it really a ninety-dollar watch?" asked Walter, with interest.

"No. I know something about watches, as I find the knowledge useful in my official capacity. The watch would be a fair bargain at forty-five dollars, but it is showy, and would readily be taken for one worth seventy-five or even ninety dollars."

"I shouldn't think the trick would pay," said the gentleman in the rear seat.

"Why not?"

"Twenty dollars isn't a large sum to be divided between two persons, especially when there's money to be paid for car fare."

"Sometimes the watch is sold for more - generally, I fancy - but the price was reduced because the purchaser was a boy. Besides, these men doubtless have other ways of making money. They are well-known confidence men. If I hadn't been on board the train our young friend would have lost his twenty dollars."

"It would have been a great loss to me," said Walter. "I am very much obliged to you, Mr. Green."

"Ah, you remember my name. Let me give you my card. Some time you may get into difficulty and want to consult me. Boys of your age are not a match for an experienced swindler."

He handed Walter a card bearing the name:

SILAS GREEN,
97 H Street.

Walter put it into his pocket with a polite expression of thanks.

Meanwhile, of course, the cars were steadily approaching Chicago. At length they entered the great Union Depot, and with the rest of the passengers Walter alighted carrying his valise in his hand.

A few feet in front of him walked Jim Beckwith, but Walter did not care to join him. He half turned, and as his glance fell on Walter he said, with a scowl: "If you ever meet me again you'll know me."

"Yes, I shall!" answered Walter, with emphasis.

CHAPTER X

AT THE INDIANA HOUSE

Walter paused before a modest hotel on Monroe Street - we will call it the Indiana House - and, entering, went up to the desk and inquired the rates of board.

"Are you commercial?" asked the clerk.

"Not at present, sir."

"We make special terms for commercial travelers. We will give you a small room on the third floor for one dollar and a half a day."

This was as cheap as Walter expected to find it at a hotel, and he signified his acceptance.

"Front!" called the clerk.

A red-haired boy about Walter's age came forward.

"Take this young man up to No. 36," said the clerk.

"Yessir," answered the bell-boy, pronouncing the two words in one.

There was no elevator in the house, and Walter

followed the boy up two flights of stairs to the third landing. The boy opened the door of a room with a small window looking out into an inner court.

"Here you are!" he said, and he put the valise on the floor.

"Thank you," said Walter.

As he spoke he drew a dime from his vest pocket and deposited it in the hand of the red-haired attendant.

The effect was magical. The bell-boy's listless manner vanished, his dull face lighted up, and his manner became brisk.

"Thank you, sir. Is there anything you want? If you do, I'll get it for you."

Walter looked about him. Soap, water, towels - all were in sight.

"Not just now," he answered, "but I am going to take a wash, and shall probably use up all the water. Some time this evening you may bring me some more."

"All right, sir. Just you ring when you want it."

He went off, and Walter was left alone. First, he took a thorough wash, which refreshed him very much after his long and dusty ride. Then he changed his linen, brushed his clothes with a hand-brush he had brought in his valise and carefully combed his hair.

"I feel a hundred per cent. better," he soliloquized. "Here I am in Chicago and now the battle of life is to begin."

Walter was sanguine and full of hope. His life had always been easy, and he did not know what it was to work for a living. Besides, the fact may as well be told - he had a very comfortable opinion of his own abilities. He felt that he was no common boy. Was he not a sophomore, or rather a junior-elect, of Euclid college? Did he not possess a knowledge more or less extensive of Latin, Greek and mathematics, with a smattering of French and German, not to speak of logic, rhetoric, etc.? For one of his age he considered himself quite accomplished, and he persuaded himself that the world would receive him at his own estimate. It would be very strange if he could not earn a living, when hundreds and thousands of his age, without a tithe of his knowledge, managed to live.

Walter went downstairs, and, as it would not be supper-time for two hours, went out to walk. He wanted to get some idea of the busy city which was for a time at least, to be his home. He walked through Monroe Street until he reached State. At the corner he caught sight of a palatial structure, nearly opposite.

"What building is that?" he asked of a boy.

"Where's year eyes?" returned the boy. "That's the Palmer House."

Walter gazed admiringly at the showy building, and wished that he could afford to put up there. It was as far ahead of the Indiana House as a city is ahead of a country village. He continued his walk until he reached the lake front, and looked with interest at the great sheet of water which spread out before him like an inland sea. He walked along the lake front for a few squares, and then, striking back into the city, saw the Tremont House, the Court-house, the Sherman house, and other handsome buildings. On his way he met hundreds of people walking briskly, and all seeming occupied.

"If all these people make a living, why shouldn't I?" he asked himself. "I think I am as smart as the average."

Secretly Walter thought himself a great deal smarter. It must be remembered that Walter was not quite eighteen - a self-conceited age - and he over-estimated his strength and ability. On the whole, it is fortunate that the young do not comprehend the difficult struggle that lies before them, or they would become discouraged before they had fairly entered upon it. It is well that they should be hopeful and sanguine. They are more likely to succeed.

Walter wandered around in a desultory way, and it was more than an hour before he reached the hotel at which he was stopping. As he entered the public room he started back in surprise, as his glance rested on a man wearing a white hat. Surely this was the man who had sold him the gold watch. How did it happen that he was not on the way to Dakota?

He coughed, with a view to attracting the attention of his railroad acquaintance.

The ruse succeeded. The man turned, and evidently recognized Walter. He looked doubtful, not having yet met his confederate nor learned how the plot had come out.

Horatio Alger, Jr.

"I believe I met you on the train," said Walter, smiling.

The smile decided the other that it would be safe to acknowledge the acquaintance.

"Yes, I remember you now."

"You sold me a watch?"

"Yes," answered the other, hesitating.

"I thought you wanted to take a train to Dakota this evening?" went on Walter.

"So I do, but it doesn't go till eight o'clock. May I ask what time it is? You know I sold you my watch."

"I suppose that is Chicago time," said Walter, pointing to a clock on the left-hand side of the office.

"I wonder whether he's got the watch still?" thought the other. "He must have, as he makes no fuss about it."

Walter was waiting cunningly to see if his railroad acquaintance would betray himself.

"I'm awfully sorry to part with the watch," he said. "If you keep it, I may buy it back some time."

"I'm sorry I can't oblige you," said Walter, "but I have sold it already."

"Sold the watch already!" ejaculated the man in the white hat. "Did you sell it since you reached Chicago?"

"No; I sold it on the train."

"You don't mean it!" exclaimed the other, in amazement. "Who did you sell it to?"

"Jim Beckwith," answered Walter.

"Jim Beckwith!"

The man in the white hat stared at Walter with an air of startled perplexity that almost made our hero laugh.

"Yes, that's what he said his name was, or rather somebody told me it was his name."

"Jim Beckwith bought that watch of you!" repeated the stranger slowly.

"Yes; do you know him?"

"I have heard of him," said the other.

"Oh, I nearly forgot to say that he claimed the watch as his - said you had stolen it from him."

"Jim Beckwith said that?"

"Yes."

And you gave it up to him?"

"Yes, but not till he paid me the twenty dollars I gave for it."

The other was more and more mystified.

Horatio Alger, Jr.

"Jim Beckwith gave you twenty dollars?" he said.

"Yes. That leaves me all right. If you want to buy it back at any time you must apply to him."

The man in the white hat stared at Walter as if he was a museum freak.

"Boy," he said, in a tone of enforced admiration, "you're smart!"

"I am glad you think so, sir," returned Walter. "You pay me a compliment."

"How old are you?"

"Seventeen."

"A seventeen-year-old boy who can get the better of Jim Beckwith is smart, and no mistake."

"Perhaps you wouldn't mind telling me whether it's true that the watch belongs to Mr. Beckwith, as he says?"

"I bought it of another man, who may have stolen it from him," said he of the white hat, cautiously.

"Well, you'll have to settle with him. I'm out of it!"

While Walter was speaking, an extraordinary change came over the countenance of the man in the white hat. The color faded from his cheeks and he half rose from his seat. He was not looking at Walter, but beyond him, toward the door. Walter turned, following his

look, and when he saw who had entered he understood
the situation.

Horatio Alger, Jr.

CHAPTER XI

THE MAN FROM DAKOTA

The man who had just entered the reading-room was no other than Detective Green.

He nodded pleasantly to Walter.

"So you have put up here," he said. "Well, it is a good place. And is this gentleman a friend of yours?" indicating the man in the white hat.

"I bought the watch from him."

"Ha! I thought so. I see you know me, Steve Ashton."

"Yes, sir," answered Ashton, nervously. "I hope you are well."

"You are very kind. Then you really hope I am well?"

"Of course. Why shouldn't I?"

"Well, there are some of your companions, I hear, who are not so cordial - Jim Beckwith, for instance. By the way, you have some business arrangements with Jim Beckwith?"

"I know him, sir," answered Astern, hesitatingly. "You know him well, I suspect. So you sold my young friend here a watch?"

"Yes, sir."

"At a remarkable sacrifice?"

"Yes, sir. It was worth more than he paid for it."

"And yet it seemed likely to be a losing bargain for him. It would have been - but for me."

Ashton looked at Walter inquiringly. The latter smiled.

"You gave me credit for being smarter than I was," said Walter. "Mr. Green, here, came to my assistance."

"I think, Mr. Ashton," said Detective Green, with suavity, "that you have a wife and family in Dakota?"

"I, sir -"

"Yes; and it was to obtain money to join them that you sold your watch on the train?"

"Yes, sir," answered Ashton, faintly.

"I am going to give you a bit of advice. It will be wise for you to go to Dakota, as you planned. This is a wicked city - in spots - and I am afraid you have been keeping bad company. How long have you known Beckwith?"

"About six months."

"And he drew you into this business?"

"Yes, sir."

"I thought so. You are new to the profession. Still, I knew you. I make it a point to get acquainted with the new men. Is the watch honestly yours?"

"Yes, sir."

"Get it back from Beckwith, and then drop his acquaintance. If necessary, leave Chicago. Have you a trade?"

"Yes, sir. I am a machinist."

"It is a good trade. Go back to it. Is that advice friendly?"

"Yes, sir," answered Ashton, with more confidence. "I didn't expect to get friendly advice from Detective Green."

"Perhaps not. You didn't know me, that was all. You looked upon me as an enemy, I suppose?"

"Yes, sir."

"I am an enemy to those who are incurably bad. I think you were meant for an honest man."

"So I was, sir. I should be still if I hadn't met with Jim Beckwith."

"Have done with him, then. If you follow my advice you need not fear meeting with me again."

The detective went up to the desk, bought a cigar and then left the room, with a nod to Ashton and Walter.

"Will you follow his advice?" asked Walter.

"Yes, I will. Hereafter I will depend upon honest work for an honest livelihood. What is your name?"

"Walter Sherwood."

"Then, Walter Sherwood, I am glad I did not succeed in robbing you. Yet I am glad I met you. It will lead to my reformation. Will you give me your hand?"

"Willingly."

Steve Ashton shook the proffered hand energetically.

"If I can do you a favor at any time I shall be glad to do so."

"Perhaps you can. I cannot afford to live at a hotel. Can you recommend me to some respectable but modest-priced boarding-house?"

"Yes. The widow of a machinist who used to be employed in the same shop as myself keeps a few boarders. I think she would take you for six dollars a week, or five if you have a friend to room with you."

"Can you show me the place after supper - that is, unless you are in a hurry to start for Dakota?" He added, with a smile.

"I never was in Dakota in my life," said Ashton. "I told you a lie."

"I was beginning to think so."

"But I shall drop all that. From this time on you can trust me."

After supper Walter went round with Ashton to a house in Harrison Street - the boarding-house referred to. The door was opened by a careworn woman of middle age.

"How do you do, Mr. Ashton?" she said, with an inquiring look.

"Very well, thank you, Mrs. Canfield. Have you any rooms vacant?"

"Are you asking for yourself?"

"No, for my young friend here, Mr. Sherwood."

"Do you want a large room or a small one?" asked Mrs. Canfield, brightening up a little.

"That depends a little on the price," answered Walter.

"I can give you a hall bedroom and board for five dollars and a half a week."

"Can you show me the room?"

"Be kind enough to follow me."

Walter followed the landlady up a narrow staircase, or rather two of them, and was shown a hall bedroom, which seemed to be uncomfortably full, though it only contained a bedstead, a chair, a very small bureau and a washstand. There was scarcely room for him to stand unless he stood on the bed. It was indeed vastly different from his nice college room and from his comfortable chamber at home.

"I should like to see a larger room," said Walter, not venturing to make any comment on the hall room.

He was shown an adjoining apartment, about ten feet by twelve. It was small, but decidedly preferable to the other.

"How much do you charge for this room, Mrs. Canfield?"

"I shall have to charge you six dollars if you occupy it alone, but if you can get another young gentleman to occupy it with you I will say ten dollars for the two."

"I will take it alone at first. Can I move in tomorrow morning?"

"I will have it ready for you by eleven o'clock."

"That will do."

"How do you like it?" asked Ashton, when they were in the street.

"I think I can make it do."

"I suppose you have been used to something better?"

"Yes."

"I can direct you to a better house."

"Thank you, but six dollars a week is all I can afford at present. I have no income, but I shall look for a place at once."

"You haven't any trade, have you?"

"No," answered Walter, with a smile. Brought up as he had been, it seemed odd to be asked if he had a trade.

"Some trades pay very well. I have a nephew who is a bricklayer. He gets from three to four dollars a day."

"I am afraid I should not like that business. Besides, it would take a good while to learn it."

Walter smiled to himself as he pictured some of his aristocratic college friends seeing him laying bricks. He was not a snob, nor would he have disdained to notice a friend or school companion filling such a position, but he felt that Providence must have something in store for him more congenial, though perhaps less lucrative.

"I have a cousin who is a carpenter," proceeded Ashton. "He makes two dollars and a half a day, and supports a wife and three children in comfort."

"I wonder if I could support a family on fifteen dollars a week?" thought Walter. "Fortunately, I have only to support myself. I ought to be able to do that in a large city like Chicago."

Reared in comfort, Walter knew very little of the competition and struggles of workingmen, and had an idea that he would be able easily to command a salary of ten dollars a week, though he was wholly disqualified for any special line of business. This he set down as the minimum. Paying six dollars a week for board, he calculated that he could get along on this salary with extreme economy. Fortunately, he was pretty well provided with clothing, or would be when he had sent for his trunk, and would not find it necessary for some time to come to purchase anything, except probably a pair of shoes, a necktie, or some trifle. Then probably his pay would soon be raised, and this would make him comfortable.

That evening Walter went to Hooley's Theater and occupied a dollar seat. It was hardly prudent, but he had seventy dollars still, and that seemed to him a large sum. He enjoyed the play, and got a sound night's rest after it.

The next morning he settled his hotel bill, took his gripsack in his hand, and walked over to his new boarding-house.

Horatio Alger, Jr.

CHAPTER XII

IN SEARCH OF EMPLOYMENT

"Wanted - A young man of seventeen or eighteen in an insurance office, No. 169 La Salle Street."

This notice attracted the attention of Walter as he ran his eyes over the advertising columns of the Chicago *Times* on the second day after his arrival in the city.

"I think that will suit me," he said to himself. "It is a nice, respectable business, and I think I should like it. I will go to the office and make inquiries."

He entered a large building, devoted to offices, and ascended to the third story, where he found the office of Perkins & Windermere, the names given in the advertisement. A young man of about his own age was coming out of the office as he entered - an unsuccessful applicant, Walter inferred.

Opening the door, he saw a man of about forty seated in a revolving chair at a desk.

"I believe you advertised for an assistant," began Walter, as the occupant of the chair turned round.

"Yes," replied Mr. Perkins - for it was he - eying

Walter with a scrutinizing glance.

"I would like to apply for the position."

"Humph! Do you know anything of the insurance business?"

"Not practically, sir."

"That's against you."

"I think I could soon familiarize myself with it so as to make myself useful."

"How old are you?"

"Very nearly eighteen."

"Do you live in Chicago?"

"I do now. I have recently come from the East."

"What education have you?"

"I spent two years at Euclid College," answered Walter, with conscious pride.

"So you are a college student?"

"Yes, sir." "Humph! That won't do you any good."

"I hope it won't do me any harm, sir," said Walter, somewhat nettled.

"No, unless it has made you conceited. I am a graduate of the People's College."

"I don't think I have heard of that, sir."

"I mean the common school. Don't think much of college myself. They don't help in our business. They didn't have any insurance companies in Greece or Rome, did they?"

"I never heard of any, sir."

"I thought not. You see, we of to-day are rather ahead of Demosthenes and Cicero, and those old fellows. I suppose Rome was quite a sizable place."

"I have always heard so," answered Walter.

"I'll bet a quarter it wasn't as big or as smart a place as Chicago. I don't believe they had any such hotel there as the Palmer House, or any dry-good store as big as Marshall Field's."

"I don't believe they did," Walter admitted.

"Did Rome ever win the baseball championship?" demanded Mr. Perkins.

"No, sir."

"I thought not. Then what's the use in spending four years over those old fellers? How is it going to help you?"

"I don't expect it will help me to earn a living, sir. Do you think you can employ me?"

"What are your ideas as to a salary, young man?"

"I thought of ten dollars," said Walter, hesitatingly.

"Ten dollars!" ejaculated Mr. Perkins. "Just what I thought. Because you've been to college you think you are worth a big salary."

"Do you call that a big salary, sir?" asked Walter, disconcerted.

"It wouldn't be if you had a couple of years' experience, but for a beginner it is simply - enormous."

"What did you expect to pay?" asked Walter, in a depressed tone.

"Five dollars is about the figure."

"I couldn't work for that, sir. It wouldn't pay my board."

"Where are you boarding - at the Palmer House?" inquired Perkins, rather sarcastically.

"No, sir. I am at a cheap boarding-house on Harrison Street, where I pay six dollars a week," answered Walter, with spirit.

"Then I don't think we can make a bargain, although I rather like your looks."

This, at any rate, was a little encouraging.

"But I can't pay your figure. I'll tell you what you'd better do."

"I shall be glad of any advice."

"Become an agent. You look as if you had a gift of the gab. A successful life insurance agent will make a good deal more than ten dollars a week."

"Can I get such a position?" asked Walter, hopefully.

"Yes. I'll employ you myself, on a commission, of course. You'll be paid according to your work I've known an agent to make a hundred and twenty-five dollars in a single week."

"If you think I can do it, sir, I'll try."

"Very well. Hare you ever studied life insurance?"

"No, sir, but I have a general idea of it."

"I will give you some documents - instructions to agents, etc. Take these home, study them, and come to me when you think you understand it well enough to talk people into it."

Mr. Perkins opened his desk, and selecting some papers handed them to Walter.

"When you come again, if there is anything you don't see into, let me know, and I'll explain it to you."

"Thank you, sir."

Walter went home and set himself to studying the insurance documents given him by Mr. Perkins. Here he found his college training of service. It was like studying a science, and Walter, who went to work systematically, soon came to understand the system, with the arguments for and against it. He made calculations of the expenses attending the different classes of life insurance, selecting the ages of thirty, forty and fifty as illustrations. The result was that when he went round to the office the next day he felt considerable confidence in his ability to talk up insurance.

Mr. Perkins seemed surprised to see him so soon.

"Do you think you understand the duties of a canvasser?" he asked.

"Yes, sir."

"You haven't devoted much time to it. You only took the documents yesterday."

"True, sir; but I have spent several hours in examining them."

"Were there any things you did not understand?"

Walter mentioned one or two points.

"Now, that I may get an idea of your working ability, suppose you try to insure me. I will take the part of an ordinary business man who is unfamiliar with the subject."

Walter was not bashful, and saw at once the value of this suggestion.

Without going into details, it may be stated that he acquitted himself very creditably.

"You surprise me," Mr. Perkins admitted. "You seem

to have made yourself quite familiar with the subject. I will take you into my employment as an agent and allow you half commission."

"Do you wish me to operate in the city?"

"It will be better for you to start outside. I will send you to Elm Bank, about fifteen miles distant. Once there, I shall leave you to your own discretion. I will pay your fare there and back, and trust to your doing something to repay me for the outlay."

"Very well, sir."

Walter took the necessary directions, and after dinner took a train out to the suburban town which I have called Elm Bank, though this is not the real name. He congratulated himself on so soon obtaining employment, though it remained to be seen how he would succeed. However, Walter was sanguine, not as yet having put himself in a position to meet the rebuffs which are sure to lie in wait for agents of any kind. He thought over his prospects with pleased anticipations. He felt that the position was much higher than that of a boy in an office. It was one usually filled by men of maturity and business experience. Besides, if successful, the rewards would be ample. The thought of the agent who made a hundred and twenty-five dollars in a single week occurred to him and encouraged him. He would have been content with a salary of ten dollars a week, but here was a business which might lead to a great deal more.

He seated himself next to a girl of sixteen, with a pleasant face and frank, cordial manner.

Presently the girl tried to raise the window - she occupied the seat next to it - but it resisted her efforts.

"Will you allow me to try?" asked Walter, politely.

"Thank you. You are very kind."

Walter leaned over and succeeded in raising it.

"Thank you," said the young lady. "I am only going to Elm Bank, but I like the fresh air, even for a short distance."

Here was a surprise for Walter.

"Are you going to Elm Bank?" he said. "So am I."

CHAPTER XIII

A YOUNG INSURANCE AGENT

"You don't live in Elm Bank?" said the young girl, inquiringly.

"No," answered Walter, swelling with pardonable pride. "I am going there on business." "Have you ever been there before?" asked his fair companion.

"No."

"You look young to be in business."

"I haven't been in business long," returned Walter, wondering if he looked so very young. Then he added, with a sudden impulse, "I am an insurance agent."

"Are you? I - I thought -"

"What did you think?" asked Walter, a little curious.

"I would rather not say it."

"I wish you would."

"You will promise not to be offended?"

"Yes."

"I have been told that insurance agents are very cheeky."

Walter laughed.

"I don't know about that," he said. "I haven't been in the business long enough yet. Do you know if any insurance agents have visited Elm Bank lately?"

"No, I don't think so."

"Perhaps you would like to have your life insured?" said Walter, with a humorous look.

"Can you insure me fifty cents' worth?"

"I am afraid not."

"Then I must put it off, for that is all the money I have."

Conversation drifted into other channels, and was kept up till the cars slowed down and the conductor, putting his head in at the door, called out, "Elm Bank."

Walter and his companion rose and, leaving the car, stepped out on the platform. Walter asked leave to carry a small bundle belonging to the young lady.

"Could you recommend any one who is likely to want his life insured?" he asked.

His companion pointed to a small house some quarter of a mile distant, but plainly visible on account of its high location.

"That house belongs to a German named Louis Fishbach," she said. "He has a little money, and earns good wages in a shoe shop. He has a wife and four young children. Perhaps he will be willing to insure."

"Thank you. I will try him."

"I will leave you here, as I live in a different direction. I am sure I am much obliged to you for your politeness, Mr. -" Here she hesitated.

"Sherwood," supplied Walter.

"Mr. Sherwood. My name is Jennie Gilbert."

"Good afternoon, Miss Jennie," said Walter, politely removing his hat.

He stopped a moment and watched the retreating figure of the young girl.

"I hope I shall meet her again some time," he said to himself.

"I say, who be you?"

Walter turned quickly, and found himself confronted by a stout, hulking young fellow, broad-shouldered, and dressed in country fashion. He was, judging from his appearance, about twenty-one years of age. His tone and face indicated that he was displeased.

"Why do you want to know?" asked Walter coldly.

"Why do I want to know? I'll tell you why I want to know. I ain't goin' to have any city dude chinning up to my best girl."

"Is Miss Jennie Gilbert your best girl?" asked Walter.

"Well, she can be if she wants to be. I picked her out a year ago, and as soon as she is old enough I'm goin' to let her know it."

"Then she isn't your best girl now?"

"No matter whether she is or not. I ain't goin' to have you paying 'tentions to her."

"I don't see what business it is of yours," retorted Walter.

"You'll find out if I give you a lickin'!" growled the other, handling the stick which he carried in a suggestive manner.

Walter was inclined to retort in kind, but all at once it struck him as foolish to get into a quarrel about a girl whom he had known less than an hour.

"If it will make you feel any better," he said, "I'll tell you that I got acquainted with Miss Gilbert in the cars this afternoon. I never met her before, and, as I live in Chicago, I don't suppose I shall ever meet her again."

The young man's face cleared up.

"Come, that's honest," he said. "I thought you wanted to cut me out."

"If Miss Gilbert likes you I shan't interfere," said Walter. "Now I'm going to talk business. I would like to insure your life."

"What's that? You ain't a doctor, be you?"

"No."

Walter proceeded to explain in as simple terms as he could command the object and methods of life insurance.

The young man scratched his head.

"When do I get the money?" he asked.

"It is paid after your death."

"Then it won't do me any good."

"No; but suppose you have a wife and children - you would like to leave them something, wouldn't you?"

"I might live longer than my wife," suggested the young man triumphantly.

Walter found that his new acquaintance could only be influenced by considerations of personal advantage, and was compelled to give up the attempt to insure him.

He kept on his way till he reached the house of Mr. Fishbach, to whom he had been recommended.

Fortunately for his purpose, the shoe shop in which the German was employed was closed for the day, and

Walter found him at home mending a wagon in the back yard.

"Good afternoon, Mr. Fishbach," said Walter, raising his hat politely.

"I don't know who you are," answered Mr. Fishbach, with a scrutinizing glance.

"I should like to insure your life."

"You want to insure my life - what's dat?"

"If you will tell me your age, I will explain to you." "I was forty-nine next Christmas. You ain't the census man, eh?"

"No; that is quite another matter. Now, Mr. Fishbach," continued Walter, referring to a pamphlet in his hand, "if you will pay to the company which I represent forty-four dollars every year, when you die a thousand dollars will be paid to your wife, or any one else you may name."

"You won't pay me till I am dead, eh?"

"No."

"How will I know you pay then?"

"We do business on the square. We keep our promises."

"You pay the money to my widow, eh?"

"Yes. If you pay twice as much we will pay two

thousand dollars."

"What good will that do me, eh?"

"You will leave your wife comfortable, won't you?"

"If she gets much money she'll maybe marry again."

"Perhaps so."

"And the money will go to her second husband, eh?"

"If she chooses to give it to him."

"By jiminy, that won't suit me. I will spend my money myself."

"But if you die, how will your wife and children get along?"

"What makes you think I'm goin' to die, eh? Do I look delicate?"

As Walter surveyed the stout, rotund figure of Mr. Fishbach he could not help laughing at the idea of his being delicate.

"You look likely to live," he was forced to admit. "Still, life is uncertain." "You can't scare Louis Fishbach, young man. My father lived till seventy-seven and my mother was seventy-five. My children can take care of themselves when I die, and they can look after the old woman."

Walter used such other arguments as occurred to him, but his German friend was not to be moved, and he rather despondently put his documents into his pocket and went out into the street.

"I had no idea I should find it so difficult," he reflected.

Life insurance seemed to him so beneficent, and so necessary a protection for those who would otherwise be unprovided for, that he could not understand how any one who cared for his wife and children could fail to avail himself of its advantages.

After leaving the house of Mr. Fishbach he kept on in the same direction. Being unacquainted in Elm Bank, he had to trust to chance to guide him.

A little distance beyond was an old-fashioned, two-story house.

"Perhaps I had better call," thought Walter, and he entered the path that led to the side door. He had scarcely taken three steps when he was startled by a scream that seemed to proceed from the interior.

"Help! help!" was the cry that reached him.

He started to run, and on reaching the door opened it without ceremony. The sight that confronted him was one to test his courage.

CHAPTER XIV

AN EXCITING ENCOUNTER

To understand the scene in which Walter became an actor a brief explanation is necessary.

The occupant of the house was a woman of perhaps thirty-five. Her husband, Ephraim Gregory, was employed in Chicago, and went to and from the city every day. It was somewhat inconvenient to live at Elm Bank, but both he and his wife were fond of the country, and were willing to submit to some inconvenience for the sake of the sweet, pure air and rural surroundings. They had one child, a little girl of five.

Twenty minutes previous Mrs. Gregory had been sitting at her sewing, with little Rosa on the floor beside her, when, without the ceremony of a knock, the outer door was opened and a tall, powerful man, whose garb and general appearance indicated that he was a tramp, entered the room.

"What do you want?" asked Mrs. Gregory, rising in alarm.

"I'm hungry," answered the tramp, in a hoarse voice.

He might be hungry, but his breath indicated that he had been drinking. Mrs. Gregory would gladly have dismissed him, but she was afraid to do so. If only her husband had been at home!

"Sit down," she said, "and I will find you something."

She went to the pantry and returned with some bread and cold meat, which she set before her uncouth visitor.

"If you will wait five minutes I will make you some tea," she said.

"I don't want any slops," said her visitor, scornfully. "Give me brandy."

"I have none."

"Then whisky, gin - anything!"

"We don't keep liquors in the house. My husband and I never drink them."

At this he swore in a manner that terrified his unwilling hostess, and anathematized her for a temperance crank. This aroused her spirit.

"If you want liquor," she said, "you may go where it is sold. I won't supply it to you or anybody else. If you want hot tea you can have it."

"Give it to me, then."

Mrs. Gregory hastened to steep some tea - she had hot water all ready - and set it before the ruffian. He ate and drank eagerly, voraciously, and did not leave a crumb behind him. He had certainly spoken the truth when he said he was hungry. Then he arose, and she hoped he would go. But he turned to her with a significant look.

"I want money," he said.

"I can give you none," she answered, her heart sinking.

"Oh, yes, you can."

"Are you a thief?" she demanded, with a flash of spirit.

"You can call me that if you like."

There was little hope of shaming him, she saw.

"Look here, missis," he went on roughly, "you've got money in the house, and I must have it."

"How do you know that I have money in the house?"

"Your husband brought some home last night. It is here now."

This was true, and she was startled to find how much this man knew.

"Do you know my husband?" she asked.

"Yes, I know him. His name is Ephraim Gregory. He had some money paid him yesterday and it is here. I don't know where it is, but you do. Get it, and be quick about it!"

Mrs. Gregory saw by this time that her visitor was a desperate villain and that she was in a critical position. He might, since he knew so much, know the amount of money which her husband had entrusted to her for safekeeping. If she could buy him off for five dollars she would do so.

"Will you go if I give you five dollars?" she asked.

He laughed.

"No, I won't. Why should I take five dollars when you have a hundred here?"

She turned pale. The worst was true, then. This man had in some mysterious manner discovered the exact sum which she had in charge. Why had not her husband kept it in his own possession? It would have been more prudent.

"I can't give you the money," she said, pale but resolute.

"Oh, yes, you will!" he answered mockingly.

"Go away, please," she said in a pleading tone. "I have given you a meal, though you had no claim on me. Let that be sufficient."

"You can't fool me!" he replied roughly. "Bring me the money, or it will be the worse for you."

"I cannot!" she gasped.

"Then, by Heaven, I'll brain you!"

As he spoke he raised the chair on which he had been sitting and held it in position above his head, ready to bring it down upon the helpless woman.

Then it was that she uttered the piercing scream which brought Walter into the house.

His astonished glance rested on the terrified woman, with her little girl clinging in alarm to her dress, cowering beneath the chair which seemed ready to descend upon her.

Walter did not hesitate a moment. Though the tramp was possessed of twice his strength, he darted forward and grasped him by the arm.

"What are you about?" he demanded sternly.

The tramp turned at the unexpected interference and partially lowered the chair.

"What business is it of yours, you impudent young jackanapes?" he growled.

"I will make it my business," said Walter, bravely. "I won't see a lady struck down by a ruffian!"

"Take care how you talk. I can twist you round my finger, you manikin!" "What does this man want?" asked Walter, turning to Mrs. Gregory.

"He demands money," was her answer.

"So he is a thief!" exclaimed Walter, contemptuously.

"I'll fix you for that!" growled the tramp, with a frown.

Walter quickly explored the room in search of a weapon, for he saw that he would have to defend himself.

There was a fireplace in the apartment, and resting beside it was a poker of large size. Walter sprang for this, and, grasping it firmly, brandished it in a threatening manner.

"Go upstairs, madam," he said, "and lock yourself in. I will attend to this man."

The tramp burst into a contemptuous laugh.

"Why, you young whippersnapper!" he said, "I could handle half a dozen boys like you."

"I don't like to leave you in the power of this man," said Mrs. Gregory. "He will kill you."

"Right you are, ma'am!"' growled the giant. "That's just what I am going to do."

The lady turned pale. She was frightened, but her concern for Walter's safety overcame her fear for herself.

"I shall stay here," she said, "It would be cowardly to leave you."

"Take my advice, boy," growled the tramp, "and clear out of here. It is no concern of yours."

Walter did not answer, but, keen, alert, vigilant, he fixed his eye warily on his formidable opponent.

"Well, youngster," said the tramp impatiently, "did you hear me?"

"Yes, I heard you."

"Leave this room, or I'll smash you!"

"Smash away!" retorted Walter.

Though he was barely five feet six inches in height, while the tramp was fully six feet, his muscles had been toughened by exercise in the college gymnasium and by rowing in the college crew, and he was wonderfully quick in his motions.

Feeling that the time for forbearance was over, and irritated beyond measure by Walter's audacity, the tramp prepared to carry out his threat. He raised the chair and with a downward sweep aimed at Walter's head.

Had the blow taken effect, this story would never have been written. But Walter's quick eye foresaw the movement, and, springing aside, he dodged the blow and brought down the poker on the muscular part of the giant's arm with what force he could command. There was a howl of pain, and the tramp's arm hung limp and lifeless at his side, while with the other he clasped it in evident suffering.

"You murderous young villain!" he shrieked. "I'll kill you for that!"

Walter felt that he was in a dangerous position.

"Leave the room, please!" he said to Mrs. Gregory.

"You will be in my way." She obeyed, for her champion had shown himself worthy to command, and Walter sprang to the other side of the table, placing it between him and his foe.

By this time the tramp had got ready for an attack. He dashed round the table after Walter, and finally succeeded, in spite of the boy's activity, in grasping him by the shoulder.

"Ah!" he said, with a deep sigh of content, "I've got you now. I'll pay you for that blow!"

Walter felt that he had never been in such a tight place before.

CHAPTER XV

THE EXCITEMENT DEEPENS

Walter was fortunate enough not to lose his head under any circumstances. He noticed that his opponent held him by his right hand, and it was his right arm which had been lamed. Naturally, therefore, it had lost some of its strength. This was his opportunity. With a sudden twist he wriggled out of the giant's grasp, and, under-standing that it was dangerous to be at too close quarters, he threw open the outer door and dashed into the yard.

Whether this would, on the whole, have helped him, was uncertain, as the tramp could probably outrun him, but just in the nick of time a team appeared, driven by a young man, perhaps twenty-five, of remarkable size. Hiram Nutt was six feet six inches in height, the tallest man in the county, and he was as athletic as he was tall. He tipped the scales at two hundred and ten pounds, and was famous for his feats of strength. He was a farmer's son and lived at Elm Bank.

When he saw Walter dash out of the house, pursued by an ill-looking tramp, he thought it high time to interfere.

"What's up?" he demanded, still retaining his seat in

the wagon.

"None of your business!" retorted the tramp, too angry to be prudent, "The kid's been impudent, and I'm going to pound him to a jelly."

Meanwhile, Walter was leading the tramp a chase round the wagon, narrowly escaping seizure.

"Help me!" exclaimed Walter, panting.

"If you do, I'll lay you out!" exclaimed the pursuer, who had been too much occupied to notice the formidable size of the young man in the wagon.

Hiram Nutt smiled - a smile of conscious strength.

"Jump in the wagon, boy!" he said. "I'll take care of you."

Walter obeyed directions, and the tramp tried to follow him.

But in an instant Hiram had risen to his full height and, leaping to the ground, hurried to the rear of the vehicle and caught hold of the tramp. The latter tried to resist, but he was like a child in the grasp of a man. He looked up in amazement, for he was proud of his strength.

"What museum did you escape from, you - monster?" he panted.

Hiram laughed.

"Never mind," he said. "It's well I'm here. Now, boy,

who is this man?"

"I found him in that house, ready to strike down the lady who lives there because she would not give him what money she had."

Hiram Nutt's brows contracted.

"Why, you thieving scoundrel!" he cried, vigorously shaking his captive, "you dared to threaten Mrs. Gregory? Did he hurt the lady?" he added anxiously.

"No; I heard her cry for help and rushed in. Then he turned upon me."

"He might have killed you!"

"I wish I had!" ejaculated the tramp, with a scowl.

"Where is Mrs. Gregory now?"

"I told her to go upstairs."

Just then the lady, who from an upper window had observed the discomfiture and capture of her enemy, came out.

"Oh, Mr. Nutt," she exclaimed, "I am so glad you came along! I was afraid this brave boy would get hurt."

"It isn't he that will get hurt now," said Nutt, significantly. "How came this fellow in your house?"

"He came in half an hour ago and asked for food."

"And you gave it to him?"

"Yes; I got ready a lunch for him and made him some tea, though he wanted liquor."

"And this was the way of repaying the favor?"

"He had heard in some way that my husband brought home some money last evening and he demanded it. I wish, Mr. Nutt, you would take charge of it till my husband comes home. I don't dare to have it in the house."

"It won't be necessary, for there comes your husband."

It was true. Ephraim Gregory turned the corner of the street, and paused in surprise at the spectacle before him.

"What's the matter, Lucy?" he asked.

She briefly explained.

"I am so glad you are at home," she sighed. "But how do you happen to come so early?"

"I think it was a presentiment of evil. I thought of the money I had left with you, and it occurred to me that it might expose you to danger. So I got leave of absence and took an early train for Elm Bank." "What shall I do with this fellow, Mr. Gregory?" asked Hiram.

"I'll go into the house and get a rope to tie him. Then we'll take him to the lock-up."

"Let me go!" said the tramp, uneasily. "I was only joking."

"You carried the joke too far, my friend," said Hiram, significantly. "I'll take you round to the lock-up - by way of joke - and Judge Jones will sentence you to the penitentiary - just to help the joke along."

"Let me go!" whined the tramp, now thoroughly subdued. "I am a poor man, and that's what led me to do wrong."

"I suppose you never indulged in such a little joke before?"

"No; this is the first time."

"Probably you are a church member when you are at home," said Hiram, in a tone of sarcasm. "You're a good man gone wrong, ain't you?"

"Yes," said the tramp.

"You look like it. Such good men as you are better off in jail."

"I'll leave town and never come back - I will, on my honor!" pleaded the tramp, earnestly.

"I don't put any confidence in what you say. Ah, here's the rope. Now, hold still, if you know what's best for yourself."

The tramp attempted resistance, but a little vigorous shaking up by his captor soon brought him to terms. In five minutes, with his hands and feet firmly tied, he was on his way to the lock-up. Mr. Gregory and Walter accompanied him in the wagon.

"Now, Mr. Sherwood," said Gregory, when their errand was completed, "I want to thank you for your brave defense of my wife."

"I only did what any one would do under the same circumstances," said Walter, modestly.

"Any one of the requisite courage. You put yourself in danger."

"I didn't think of that, Mr. Gregory."

"No, I suppose not, but it is proper that I should think of it. You have placed me under an obligation that I shall not soon forget. You must do me the favor to come home to supper with me and pass the night. Will it interfere seriously with your business?"

"I am a life-insurance agent," said Walter, "or, at least, I am trying to be, but have not yet succeeded in writing a policy."

"I have been thinking of insuring my life for a small sum. If you come home with me you may talk me into doing it."

"Then I will certainly accept your invitation," said Walter, smiling.

"My wife made me promise to keep you. She wants to show her gratitude. Besides, you may be wanted to appear against the prisoner to-morrow morning."

"I shall be glad to help him to his deserts," said Walter. "The sooner he is locked up the better it will be for the community."

Horatio Alger, Jr.

Walter had no reason to regret his acceptance of the invitation. Mrs. Gregory exerted herself to the utmost in providing an appetizing supper, far in advance of anything he would have had set before him at his boarding-house, Mrs. Canfield being an indifferent cook. Generally her butter was strong and her tea weak, while the contrary should have been the case, and her biscuit heavy with saleratus. Walter thoroughly enjoyed his supper, and was almost ashamed of his appetite. But it gave his hostess great pleasure to see his appreciation of the meal, and she took it as a compliment to herself as a cook.

After supper Walter and Mr. Gregory sat down to business. He explained the methods of the insurance company for which he was acting as agent, and found Mr. Gregory an interested and intelligent listener.

"You may write me a policy for a thousand dollars," he said.

"You will need to pass a medical examination," said Walter.

"Certainly; will our village physician do?" "Yes."

"Then take your hat and walk over with me. It is only half-a-mile distant."

The whole matter was adjusted that evening, and Walter was pleased to feel that he had made a successful start in his new business.

The next morning the tramp was brought before Justice Jones, who arranged to hold court early to oblige Walter and Mr. Gregory, and the prisoner received a sentence of a year's confinement. He gave the name of Barney Fogg, and under that name received his sentence. He scowled fiercely while Walter was giving his evidence, and as he was taken from the court-room handcuffed, he turned toward our hero and said: "It's your turn now, young bantam, but I'll be even with you yet."

"What a terrible man!" said Mr. Gregory, shuddering. "I hope I shall never see him again."

CHAPTER XVI

WALTER GOES INTO A NEW BUSINESS

One swallow doesn't make a summer, and one policy doesn't establish the success of an insurance agent. Walter received from Mr. Perkins five dollars commission on the policy he had written at Elm Bank, and this encouraged him to renewed efforts. But in the fortnight following he only succeeded in writing a policy for two hundred and fifty dollars, for a man who designed it to meet his funeral expenses. For this Walter received one dollar and a quarter. He made numerous other attempts, but he found, though he understood the subject thoroughly, that his youth operated against him. He decided that he was wasting his time, and one morning he waited on Mr. Perkins and resigned his agency.

"Have you anything else in view?" asked that gentleman.

"No, sir."

"Then why don't you keep on till you have secured another position?"

"Because it takes up my time, and prevents my getting anything else."

"I don't know but you are right, Mr. Sherwood. You have made a good beginning, and if you were ten years older I think you would make a successful agent."

"I can't afford to wait ten years," returned Walter, with a smile.

"If ever you want to come back, I will start you again."

Walter thanked Mr. Perkins, and left the office.

He now began to explore the columns of the daily papers, in the hope of finding some opening, but met with the usual rebuffs and refusals when he called upon advertisers.

At length he saw the following advertisement in the Chicago *Tribune:*

"WANTED - A confidential clerk at a salary of fifteen dollars per week. As a guarantee of fidelity, a small deposit will be required. LOCKE & GREEN, No. 257 1-2 State Street."

"Fifteen dollars a week!" repeated Walter hopefully. "That will support me very comfortably. If I get it I will change my boarding-place, for I don't like Mrs. Canfield's table. I shall feel justified in paying a little more than I do now."

The only thing that troubled him was as to the deposit. Though he had economized as closely as he knew how, he had made quite an inroad upon his small capital, and had only forty-six dollars left. He had been in Chicago four weeks, and had not yet been able to write home that he had found a permanent position. He had written about his insurance agency, and had not failed to chronicle his first success.

This letter Doctor Mack had read to his housekeeper, Miss Nancy Sprague.

"Well, Nancy," he said, "Walter is at work."

"You don't say so, doctor! What is he doing?"

"He is a life-insurance agent."

"Is that a good business?"

"Walter writes that one agent is making a hundred and twenty-five dollars a week," answered the doctor, with a humorous twinkle in his eye.

"I'm glad Master Walter has got such a good business," said the housekeeper, brightening up. "That's a great sum for a boy like him to make."

"It isn't he that has made it, Nancy. There are very few that do, and those have to be old and experienced men."

"Well, he'll make a good living, anyhow."

"Perhaps so," answered the doctor dubiously, for he understood better than Nancy how precarious were the chances of an inexperienced agent. He was not at all surprised when Walter wrote later that though he had met with some success, he thought it better to look for a situation with a regular salary attached.

"He's gaining a little knowledge of the world," thought

the guardian. "I don't think he'll be able to indulge in luxurious living for the present. It won't be long, probably, before he runs out of money."

It was with a hopeful spirit that Walter started for the office of Locke & Green. He was pretty well acquainted with Chicago by this time, and had no difficulty in locating any office in the business part of the city.

No indication was given in the advertisement of the business carried on by Locke & Green. As to that, however, Walter felt indifferent. His chief concern was the weekly salary of fifteen dollars, which he needed very much.

Arrived at the number indicated, Walter ran upstairs, and with some difficulty found the office in a small room on the fourth floor. A card on the door bore the names:

LOCKE & GREEN

Again there was no clue to the business carried on by the firm.

Walter was not sure whether he ought to knock, but finally decided to open the door and enter. He found himself in a room scarcely larger than a small bedroom, with a small desk in one corner. At this sat a man with long hair, industriously writing in a large blank book. He glanced at Walter as the door opened.

"Wait a moment, young man!" he said, in a deep bass voice. "I will be at leisure in two minutes."

He wrinkled up his face, turned back several pages,

appeared thoughtfully considering some problem, and then wrote again rapidly.

Finally he turned - he was seated in a revolving chair - and placing his two hands together, palms inward, said abruptly: "Well, young man, what can I do for you?"

"I believe you advertised in the *Tribune* this morning for a confidential clerk?"

"Yes."

"I should like to apply for the position, if it is still vacant."

"We have not yet filled the place," said Mr. Locke. "We have had several applications, but the post is a very responsible one, and we are, of course, very particular."

"I am afraid my chance is very small, then," thought Walter.

"Still, I like your appearance, and it is possible that you may suit. Have you business experience?"

"Not much, sir. Indeed, till a short time since I was a college student."

"Yale or Harvard?"

"No, sir; Euclid College."

"Ahem; small, but very respectable. Your name?"

"Walter Sherwood."

"How long were you in college?"

"Two years."

"Left of your own accord?" "Oh, yes, sir."

"Just so. I thought perhaps you might have been suspended or expelled."

"I can refer you on that point to the president or any of the professors."

"Oh, I will take your word for it."

"I left college on account of losing my property."

"Ah, indeed!" said Mr. Locke doubtfully. "Perhaps you noticed that we require a small deposit as a guarantee of fidelity."

"Yes, sir. I have a little money."

Mr. Locke looked relieved.

"Of course," continued he loftily, "doing the business we do, money is of comparatively little importance to us, except as a guarantee of fidelity. How much did you say you had?"

"I didn't say, sir. I could deposit twenty-five dollars with you."

Mr. Locke shrugged his shoulders.

"That is very little," he said.

"True, sir, but it is a good deal to me. It will be enough to insure my fidelity."

"We had a young man here this morning," said Mr. Locke musingly, "who was willing to deposit a hundred dollars with us."

"Indeed, sir! I wonder you did not take him."

"We should, so far as the money went, but I could see by his appearance that there was no business in him. Our clerk must be quick, sharp, alert. The young man was very much disappointed."

"I couldn't deposit any such sum as that, Mr. Locke."

"It will not be necessary. Still, twenty-five dollars is very small. You couldn't say thirty, could you? That is merely equal to two weeks' salary."

"Yes, sir. I might be willing to deposit thirty dollars. May I ask what business you are interested in?"

"We have control for the Western States of a valuable patent - a folding-table - and we have several hundred agents out, who report in general by letter." "That accounts for the small office," thought Walter.

"Come here a moment, and I will give you an idea how we carry on business. Here, for instance, is a page devoted to B. Schenck. He is operating for us in Minnesota. You will observe that his remittances for the last four weeks aggregate three hundred and sixty-seven dollars. He has been doing very well, but we have others who do better. On the next page is our account with G. Parker. His month's work amounts to two hundred and eighty-nine dollars."

"What would my duties be, sir?"

"To keep the office when I am out, receive letters, and answer them, and see agents."

"I think I could do that, sir."

"Hours from nine to five. I think you will suit me. If at the end of the week I don't find you satisfactory, I will pay you your wages and return your money."

"Very well, sir. I accept the position."

"You may as well hand me the money, and go to work to-day." Walter drew out thirty dollars, the greater part of his little store, and handed it to Mr. Locke.

Mr. Locke tucked it carelessly into his vest pocket, and taking his hat said: "Sit down here, and if any agents come in, tell them I will be back at one o'clock. That is all you will need to do to-day."

CHAPTER XVII

WALTER'S VISITORS

Walter sat down at the desk complacently. He had parted with thirty dollars, but it was on deposit with his new employer, and would be returned to him whenever his engagement terminated. He only hoped that his services would prove satisfactory. He meant to do his best. On fifteen dollars a week he could live very comfortably, and even save money. He felt that it would be prudent to do this, as he did not wish to call upon his guardian for any remittances during the year.

"I sha'n't have to work very hard," thought Walter.

In default of any other employment he looked over the large ledger committed to his charge. It appeared to contain certain accounts with different agents, all of whom seemed to be meeting with very good success, judging from the amount of remittances credited to them.

In about half-an-hour there was a knock at the door.

"Come in!" called out Walter.

A man of about thirty-five entered briskly. He was rather shabbily dressed, and his red face indicated possible indulgence in intoxicating liquor. "Is Mr. Locke in?" he asked.

"No, sir."

"I wanted to see him."

"I am his confidential clerk," said Walter proudly. "Are you an agent?"

"Yes, I am an agent. I suppose I ought to see him."

"He will be back at one o'clock."

"I can't stop, as I have been away for some weeks and want to go out and see my family at Barrington."

"If you wish to leave any message I will give it to Mr. Locke as soon as he returns."

"Perhaps that will do. My name is Jerome Grigson. Tell Mr. Locke I have met with excellent success in Ohio. In the last four weeks I have sold goods to the amount of four hundred and seventeen dollars."

"I should think it was doing remarkably well," observed Walter.

"It is; but any one could sell for Locke business chiefly in Mr. Locke's hands. How long have you been in the office?"

"Not long," answered Walter, who did not care to admit that his term of service covered less than an hour.

"You've a good place with a rising firm. Mind you keep it!"

"I will try to," said Walter earnestly.

"They're square men, Locke & Green. I never worked for squarer men."

This was pleasant to hear. Walter felt that he Had made no mistake in parting with his thirty Dollars.

"Well, I must be going. Have you taken down my name?"

"Yes, sir; Jerome Grigson."

"Right. Say, I will look in some time to-morrow and bring in a check for four hundred and seventeen dollars.

"Very well, sir."

Mr. Grigson left the office. Twenty minutes Later a boy of about his own age opened the door. He glanced at Walter diffidently.

"You advertised for a confidential clerk," he said. "Is - is the place filled?"

"Yes," answered Walter, in a tone of satisfaction.

"You don't want anybody else, do you?" asked the youth, looking disappointed. "Not at present, but we might be able to employ you as an agent." "Is it hard work?

"Well, of course you will have to exert yourself," said Walter condescendingly, toying with a pen as he spoke, "but successful men can earn good wages with us."

He was talking as if he was one of the partners, but it is a way young clerks have.

"Are yon one of the firm?" asked the young man doubtfully.

"No," answered Walter, "not exactly. Mr. Locke will be in about one o'clock, and if you will come round a little after that you can talk with him about an agency. I will put in a good word for you," he added, in a patronizing tone.

"Thank you, sir. I'd like to get a place."

The youth departed and Walter was left alone. But not for long. A middle-aged man entered and looked inquiringly at Walter.

"Are you Mr. Green?" he asked.

"No, sir."

"I have seen Mr. Locke, but I thought you might be Mr. Green."

Walter felt flattered to be taken for one of the firm.

"I am the confidential clerk," he said. "Can I do anything for you?"

"I wanted to see Mr. Locke and pay him some money."

"I will take it and receipt for it," said Walter briskly.

"Well, I suppose that will do, as you are the clerk."

"What name?" asked Walter, opening the book.

"Jonas Damon. Here is a check on the Corndish National Bank of Illinois for two hundred and twenty-seven dollars. I have made it payable to Locke & Green."

"All right," said Walter, in a businesslike tone.

"If you wish to see Mr. Locke he will be in at one o'clock," he added, as he put the check in his vest pocket.

"No, I am obliged to go out of town in half-an-hour. It isn't necessary to see him. He would rather see the check."

Mr. Damon laughed, and so did Walter. It Made him feel quite like a business man to be installed in an office, receiving and crediting checks.

"Have you been long in our employment?" he asked.

"About six months."

"I hope you have found it satisfactory?"

"Yes, I have made an excellent living. How much salary do you get?"

"Fifteen dollars a week," answered Walter rather complacently.

"You look like a smart young fellow. You'd easily make double the money as an agent."

"Thank you for the suggestion. I may undertake that some time. I have been a life-insurance agent."

"Did it pay?"

"Not as well as I hoped. I think I shall like my present place better."

"I must be going. Tell Mr. Locke I will be in to-morrow."

"All right."

"It is evident," thought Walter, "that I am in the employ of a substantial and prosperous firm. The duties are certainly very light and pleasant. I am in luck to get a clerkship here. It is rather surprising Mr. Locke didn't ask for references."

Then it occurred to him that the deposit was taken as a substitute for references. Then again Walter flattered himself that his personal appearance might have produced a favorable impression upon his employer and had some influence in leading to an engagement.

His next caller was a young man, dark and sallow, with a slight mustache.

"Is this the office of Locke & Green?" he asked.

"Yes, sir."

"Will you describe Mr. Locke to me?" asked the young

man, who appeared to be laboring under some excitement.

Walter was rather surprised at such a request, but complied with it.

"Yes, he's the man," said his visitor, slapping his hands together impetuously. "He's the man that cheated me out of fifty dollars!"

"You must be mistaken," said Walter. "How did he cheat you out of it?"

"One moment - are you his confidential clerk?"

"Yes."

"I thought so," returned the young man, laughing wildly. "So was I."

"You were his clerk?"

"Yes, for two weeks. I paid him fifty dollars good money as security."

"You did?" repeated Walter, with some anxiety.

"Yes; at the end of two weeks he told me I would not suit."

"But he paid you your wages and returned you your money?"

"No, he didn't!" exploded the young man. "He told me to come round on Monday morning and he would pay me."

"Well?"

"I called Monday, and he was gone! He had moved, the scoundrel! I should like to choke him!"

"Was it this office?"

"No. Let me see that book! Ah, it is the same that I kept. Have you, too, given him money?"

"I deposited thirty dollars."

"Ah, it is the same old game! You will never see a cent of it again."

"But," said Walter, "I don't understand. He is doing a good business. I have had calls from two of his agents. One of them handed me this check," and he drew out the check Mr. Damon had given him.

The young man took it and laughed bitterly.

"I don't believe there is any such bank," he said. "I never heard of it."

"Then why should the agent hand me the check?"

"To pull wool over your eyes. These agents are in league with this man Locke. That wasn't his name when he engaged me."

"What was it then?"

"He called himself Libby. Libby & Richmond, that was the name of the firm."

"What made you think he might have changed his name?"

"Because the advertisement reads the same."

"And you really think it is the same man?"

"Yes, I feel sure of it."

"He will be back at one o'clock. If you will wait till then you can see for yourself."

"I'll wait!" said the young man, grinding his teeth. "I will confront the swindler face to face. I will demand my money."

The door opened and some one put in his head, but before Walter or his visitor could see who it was it closed again.

Fifteen minutes later a telegraph boy entered the office.

CHAPTER XVIII

WALTER IS TURNED ADRIFT

"Mr. Sherwood?" said the telegraph messenger inquiringly.

"That is my name," answered Walter.

"A message for you."

Walter opened the note, and read as follows:

"I am called out of the city. You may close up at four, and leave the key with the janitor. Report for duty to-morrow morning. LOCKE."

"What is it?" asked the young man eagerly.

Walter showed him the note.

"It looks to me like some trick," said the stranger.

"But I don't see any object in it."

"He has your thirty dollars."

"And I have a check for over two hundred."

Horatio Alger, Jr.

"I would rather have the thirty dollars. What shall you do?"

"There is nothing to do but follow directions."

The young man shrugged his shoulders.

"Then you will come round to-morrow morning?" he said.

"Certainly."

"I'll look in upon you. I want to see this Mr. Locke, though I doubt if that is his name."

Walter was disposed to think the young man too suspicious. He was of a sanguine temperament, and he tried to persuade himself that there was really no good reason to suspect Mr. Locke of unfair dealing. He laid considerable stress upon the favorable reports of the agents who had called upon him during the day.

At length four o'clock came, and he closed up the office, leaving the key with the janitor. He went home, not quite knowing whether he was to be congratulated or not. He decided not to say anything just yet about his engagement, lest it might turn out to be deceptive. Had he been quite sure that it was substantial and to be relied upon, he would have written to his guardian to announce the good news, but he thought it best to wait.

The next morning he went to the office, arriving at the hour agreed upon.

"Please give me the key to Locke & Green's office," he said to the janitor.

"Mr. Locke's given up the room," was the startling reply.

Walter was dismayed.

"Given up the room! Have you seen him?" he inquired.

"Yes."

"When?"

"He called yesterday afternoon, an hour after you went away, and got the key from me. In about ten minutes he came down again, carrying a ledger in his hand.

"'I have taken another office,' he said. 'This is not large enough for me.'

"'Have you told your clerk?' I asked him.

"'Yes, I have sent a message to him,' he replied carelessly."

Walter sank against the door. He felt limp and helpless. Mr. Locke had gone off, and carried his thirty dollars with him. There was hardly room to doubt that it was a case of deliberate swindling.

True, he had the check in his possession - a check for two hundred and twenty-seven dollars - but, even if it were genuine, it was made out in favor of Locke & Green, and would be of no service to him, though in that case it would insure Mr. Locke's calling upon him. Should such be the Case, he determined that he would not give up the Check till his thirty dollars were returned.

Walter walked slowly out of the building. When he reached Dearborn Street he went into the office of a private banker, and, showing the check, asked, "Is there any such bank as this?"

"I never heard of any," said the banker.

Walter turned pale.

"Then you think it is bogus?"

"Very likely. Under what circumstances did you receive it?"

Walter explained.

"I am sorry to say that you are probably the victim of a confidence man, or firm. I think I saw an expose of some similar swindlers in the *Inter-Ocean* a few weeks since. Did you give the fellow any money?"

"Yes, sir; thirty dollars."

"You will have to whistle for it, in all probability."

Walter's heart felt as heavy as lead. He had less than twenty dollars now, and his small balance would last him less than three weeks. What should he do then? Should he write to his guardian for more money? He hated to do this, and, above all, he hated to confess that he had been victimized.

In the next three days he answered several advertisements, and made personal applications for employment. But no one seemed to want him. In one case he was offered three dollars a week as an office boy, but he had not got quite so low down as to accept this place and salary. It struck Walter as very singular that one who had spent two years at college, and possessed a fair knowledge of Latin, Greek, and mathematics, should be in so little request. He envied the small office boys whom he saw on the street, and even the busy newsboys, who appeared to be making an income. They had work to do, and he had none. He decided that he must reduce his expenses, and accordingly hired a poor hall-bedroom for a dollar and a quarter a week, and took his meals at restaurants.

One day he went into Kinsley's restaurant, on Adams Street, feeling the need of a good meal, and sat down at a table. He gave his order, and ate his dinner with appetite. He was about to rise from the table when, casting his eye about the room, he started in surprise, as at a neighboring table he saw the familiar face of Mr. Jonas Damon, whose check he held in his pocket.

Instantly his resolve was taken. He would speak to Mr. Damon, and try to ascertain something about the check.

He walked over to the table, and touching Damon on the shoulder, said: "Mr. Damon, I believe?"

The man looked up quickly, and a little change in his countenance showed that he recognised Walter; but he assumed a stolid look, and said: "Were you speaking to me, young man?"

"Yes, sir."

"What did you call me?"

"Mr. Damon."

"You're off the track. That isn't my name."

"Perhaps not," said Walter resolutely; "but when you called at Locke & Green's office and handed me a check you said your name was Jonas Damon."

"Ho, ho!" laughed Damon. "So I gave you a check, did I?"

"Yes, for two hundred and twenty-seven dollars."

"That's news to me. I'm not in a position to give such checks as that."

"I have got the check with me now."

"Why didn't you cash it?"

"It was not made payable to me."

"Then why didn't you give it to the party it was made out to?"

"Because he disappeared."

"That's a strange story. Do you know what I think?"

"No; but I should like to."

"I think you are a confidence man, and are trying to take in a poor countryman. But I've read about you fellows in the papers, and I am on my guard. You'd better go away, or I may call a policeman."

This certainly was turning the tables on Walter with a vengeance. For a fellow like Damon to accuse him of being a confidence man was something like the wolf's charge against the lamb in AEsop's fable.

Damon saw that Walter looked perplexed, and followed up the attack.

"If anybody has given you a check," he said, "I don't see what you've got to complain about. You'd better make use of it if you can."

"Do you deny that your name is Damon?"

"Of course I do. My name is Kellogg - Nelson Kellogg, of Springfield, Illinois. I am in the city to buy goods."

"And you don't know Mr. Locke, of Locke & Green?"

"Never heard of the gentleman. If you've got a check of his, you'd better advertise for him. I wish my name was Locke. I shouldn't mind receiving it myself."

Here the waiter came up with Mr. Damon's order, and that gentleman addressed himself to disposing of it.

Walter left the restaurant slowly, and walked in a dejected manner in the direction of the Palmer House. He began to think that he was a failure. When he was a student of Euclid College he was in his own estimation, a person of importance. Now he felt his insignificance. If the world owed him a living, it seemed doubtful if it was inclined to pay the debt.

CHAPTER XIX

WALTER MEETS PROFESSOR ROBINSON

Two weeks passed. Walter applied for all sorts of situations, but obtained no engagement. Meanwhile his money steadily diminished, till he awoke one morning to find only seventy-five cents in his purse. Things were getting decidedly serious.

"I wonder if there is any poorhouse in Chicago," thought Walter, not wholly in jest. "It is not the sort of home I should prefer, but it is better than genteel starvation."

He went out, breakfasted, and at the restaurant picked up a copy of the Chicago *Times*. This was a piece of luck, for it saved him from the small expenditure necessary to secure it. He turned to the department of Help Wanted, and looking down the column came to this notice:

"WANTED - By a traveling lecturer, a young man who can make himself generally useful; one who plays the violin preferred. Apply to PROFESSOR ROBINSON, Hotel Brevoort."

Walter knew this hotel. It was located on Madison Street, and was on the European plan.

"That will suit me," he said to himself. "I must lose no time in making application. I can play the violin fairly well. If it will help me to a position, I will bless the violin."

In ten minutes he was at the hotel, inquiring for Professor Robinson.

"He is in his room," said the clerk, "You can go up at once."

Guided by a bell-boy, Walter reached the door of No. 65 and knocked.

"Come in!" said a deep bass voice.

Opening the door he found himself in the presence of a stout man, inclined to be tall, with a long, full beard, who glanced at him inquiringly.

"Professor Robinson, I believe?" said Walter.

"I am the man," answered the professor.

"I have come to apply for a position. I have read your advertisement in the *Times*."

"Just so! Let me look at you."

Walter blushed a little while the professor transfixed him with his glittering eye. He anxiously hoped that he would bear inspection.

"Humph! I think you'll do. How old are you?"

"Eighteen."

In fact, Walter's birthday had been passed in Chicago.

"You are rather young. Can you play on the violin?"

"Yes, sir."

"Let me hear you."

The professor pointed to a violin on the bed.

"I am glad he doesn't expect me to furnish the violin," Walter said to himself.

He took the instrument from its case, and trying the strings began to play a series of familiar airs. The violin was not a Stradivarius, but it was of good quality, and responded satisfactorily to the efforts of the young musician. Professor Robinson listened attentively, and nodded his approval.

"You play better than the last young man I had."

Walter was glad to hear it.

"I may as well tell you the nature of your duties, in case I engage you. I call myself a traveling lecturer, but this may convey an erroneous idea. I am the discoverer of Professor Robinson's Liquid Balm, which is warranted to cure more diseases than any other patent preparation in existence. I won't go into particulars, for these can be read in my circular. Now, it is my custom to go from one town to another, engage a hall if the weather requires, otherwise gather a crowd around me in a public place, and lecture about the merits of my remarkable preparation. You, besides assisting me in a general way, are expected to draw and entertain the crowd by your performance on the violin. Can you sing?"

Walter shook his head.

"I am afraid," he said, "that if I should undertake to sing it would drive away the crowd."

"Very well! It isn't necessary, though it would have helped. Now, what are your ideas as to compensation?"

As the professor spoke, he leaned back in his chair and awaited a reply.

"I hardly know what it would be right to ask," returned Walter hesitatingly. "How much did you pay your last assistant?"

"I paid him fifteen dollars a month and his traveling expenses."

This was a good deal more than Walter had made since he had undertaken to earn his own living, yet there seemed small chance of laying up anything out of it.

"May I ask, sir," he inquired, "do you meet with pretty good success in disposing of your balm?"

"Yes; the public knows a good thing when it is brought to its attention."

"Would you be willing to pay my expenses and ten per cent. commission on sales?"

"Why do you prefer this to a stated salary?"

"Because it would be an incentive to do my best. Then if I helped you to a successful sale I should be paid in proportion."

"I have an idea. You look blooming and healthy. Are you willing I should advertise you as one who has been snatched from death by my celebrated balm?"

"I don't think I would like it, sir. It would be imposing upon the public."

"I merely suggested it, but I won't insist upon it. I suppose you are thoroughly honest and reliable?"

Walter smiled.

"I don't know that my assurance will satisfy you, but I can truly say that I am."

"You look it, and I trust a good deal to appearances. I will accept your assurance."

"Thank you, sir."

"Can you join me at once?"

"Yes, sir."

"Then I will expect you to bring your baggage here during the day - the sooner the better. You will then receive your instructions."

Walter was very glad to hear this, for his purse was so nearly exhausted that it was comforting to think his lodging and meals would hereafter be paid by some one else. When he came to reflect upon the nature of his duties - general assistant to a quack doctor, playing on village commons and in country halls to draw a crowd of prospective customers, he felt that it was hardly a thing to be proud of. With his college training he ought to be qualified for something better, but the cold, hard fact stared him in the face that it was the only employment that offered, and he must accept it or starve. Walter had become practical. His limited acquaintance with the world had made him so, and he was not going to refuse bread and butter because it was offered by a quack doctor.

Within an hour Walter had given up his room - the rent had been paid in advance - and transferred his luggage to the Hotel Brevoort, where he was assigned a small apartment on the upper floor.

"I shall leave the city in two days," said the professor. "I have put an advertisement into the daily papers which brings customers to the hotel, but I depend chiefly upon my sales on the road."

"Do you travel on the cars?" asked Walter.

"No; I have a neat wagon in which I carry a supply of bottles of balm, and this enables me to stop where I like. I prefer villages to very large towns and cities. It is better for me to visit places where there are no drugstores, as the people are more dependent on what is brought to them."

"When you are in the city shall I get my commission?"

"Ahem! I am not clear as to that," answered Professor Robinson thoughtfully. "You see you are not called upon to play."

"Suppose you give me five per cent. in Chicago and large places."

"Very well. I will do so. I will settle with you at the end of every week, if that will be satisfactory."

"Yes, sir."

Two days afterward a light wagon drew up in front of the hotel, drawn by a strong horse, and Walter helped the professor to put a trunk of medicine in the back part. Then he seated himself with Professor Robinson on the front seat, and they set out in the direction of the suburbs.

A new life was opening before Walter. What it would lead to he could not guess. At any rate, it promised him a living, and this was a practical advantage which he had learned to appreciate.

"How long have you been in this business, professor?" he asked.

"Ten years," answered the professor.

"How did you happen to go into it?"

"I'll tell you. Ten years ago I found myself in a tight place. I was on my uppers, as the actors say. A friend, who was a drug clerk, gave me the recipe for my balm, I borrowed a hundred dollars, had a quantity made up, and set out on the road."

"And now?"

"Now I am worth fifteen thousand dollars, well

invested, and can make a good living every year."

All this was encouraging to Walter. He was eager to begin his work.

CHAPTER XX

ON THE ROAD

On a small common, near the center of the village of Brandon - for special reasons I do not give the real names of places visited by the travelers - Professor Robinson halted his wagon and signed to Walter to commence playing.

"Give 'em something popular," he said.

Walter struck up "Annie Rooney," and followed it up with "McGinty."

Within ten minutes fifty persons were gathered about the wagon. Then the professor held up his hand and Walter stopped.

"Gentlemen," began the professor, "my young assistant will soon charm you again with the dulcet strains of his violin. But it is necessary for me to combine business with pleasure, and it affords me satisfaction to call your attention to the surpassing merits of my Liquid Balm, only twenty-five cents a bottle. It is a sovereign remedy for most of the diseases that flesh is heir to. All diseases of the stomach, liver, and lungs are, if not cured, very greatly mitigated by this wonderful medicine. It is the only remedy for consumption that can be relied upon. Why, gentlemen, a year since I was selling in a small town in Ohio. Among those who gathered about me was a hollow-cheeked man with a churchyard cough. He asked me if I would undertake to cure him. I answered that I would guarantee nothing, but was convinced that his life would be prolonged by the use of my balm. He bought half-a-dozen bottles. Where do you think that man is now?"

Voice in the crowd: "In the grave."

"Not a bit of it, gentlemen. He is hale and hearty, his face is full, his color healthy, and he tips the scales at one hundred and seventy-five pounds. I was myself surprised at the extraordinary efficacy of my wonderful medicine. He used in all a dozen bottles, giving me a second order later on, and so for the paltry sum of three dollars was drawn back from the brink of the grave, and restored to life and health. Now, who will buy a bottle?"

This appeal sold eight bottles.

A saffron-faced man came forward and asked if the balm could cure liver-complaint.

"My friend," said the professor, "if you will try the balm - you ought to have half-a-dozen bottles, as it is uncertain when I shall come this way again - your liver will become O. K. and your face will be as fresh and blooming as that of a twelve-year-old boy."

This prospect seemed so encouraging that the saffron-faced man bought four bottles, and took the professor's address.

At the end of about twenty minutes Walter struck up again, a lively dancing tune, and was listened to with evident pleasure.

When all who desired the balm seemed to have invested, the professor brought out a supply of toilet soaps, and sold to the amount of a couple of dollars.

At the end of two hours he packed up his wares, Walter took a seat beside him, and they started for the next village.

"You had a pretty good sale, professor," said Walter.

"Yes; as well as I can calculate I took in about ten dollars."

Walter reflected with pleasure that his commission would amount to a dollar.

The professor had another way of utilizing remedies. When he put up for the night at a hotel, he usually succeeded in paying a part of his hotel bill in medicine or toilet articles. As his average profits on the former were seventy per cent., and on the latter forty, it may be seen that this was greatly to his advantage. Walter did not wonder that he had already accumulated a small competence.

On the fourth evening, as Walter was leaving the supper-table, a tall young man, looking something like the stock pictures of Uncle Sam, came up to him.

"Say, young fellow," he commenced, "some of us young people are going to have a dance at the schoolhouse hall, but we haven't got no fiddler. Peter

Jackson, who generally plays for us, has got the lumbago and can't play. What'll you charge?"

"What do you generally pay Mr. Jackson?" asked Walter.

"Three dollars an evening."

"Do you think I can play as well as he?"

"You kin play enough sight better. He can't play no tunes that ain't fifty years old."

"Very well, I will charge you the same, that is, if the professor doesn't object."

"Go ahead and see him and let me know."

Walter sought the professor and laid the matter before him.

"All right!" was the answer. "I've no objection. You can give me one-third of the money and keep the rest yourself. Is that satisfactory?"

"Perfectly so, sir." Walter played till one o'clock. He felt rather tired when he got through, but he saw that he was making a favorable impression, and the two dollars which he would receive for himself would be of great service.

The man who first spoke to him paid him the money.

"I hope I gave satisfaction," said Walter.

"Yes, you did, and no mistake; but some of the girls

were sorry they couldn't have you for a partner."

Walter blushed.

"I am afraid," he said, "that I couldn't play and dance, too."

At his age few young men are indifferent to the favorable opinion of young ladies, and Walter would have been glad to have participated in the dancing. However, just at present, money was more acceptable to him than anything else.

When the week was concluded, the professor looked over his accounts and ascertained that Walter's commission amounted to nine dollars and sixty cents. The two dollars he had received for outside services carried his week's earnings to nearly twelve dollars.

He had been out with Professor Robinson a month when he had a surprise. It was in the town of Glenwood. His violin drew the usual crowd, who were listening with complimentary attention, when a young man, who casually paused to judge of the musician's merits, started in amazement.

"By Jove!" he exclaimed to a young lady who accompanied him. "That's my classmate, Sherwood."

"What do you mean, Hugh?" asked the young lady.

"I mean that the young man who is playing the violin is my college classmate, Walter Sherwood."

"But what on earth can have put him in such a position? Is he poor?"

"He had the reputation of being rich in college, but I remember that at the close of the sophomore year he was reported to have lost his money."

"He is nice-looking!" said the young lady, after a critical examination of Walter.

"Yes, and he's no end of a nice fellow. I am truly sorry that he is so reduced."

"Shall you go and speak to him?"

"Yes; but I shall have to wait till he is at leisure."

"Then I will go home by myself and leave you to confer together; and, by the way, Hugh, you know we are to have a little company to-night. Do you think your friend would play for us? He really plays uncommonly well."

"I will invite him as a guest. I shouldn't want to treat him as a professional performer. We can afford to treat him as an equal, for he is of good family, and brought up as a gentleman."

"I am quite willing to receive him as such."

Hugh Longwood remained in the crowd, and when the playing was over pushed up to the wagon. Walter was assisting the professor in serving out bottles of the famous balm.

"You may give me a bottle, Walter," said Longwood.

"By gracious, Hugh Longwood!" exclaimed Walter. "Who would have expected to see you here?"

"This is my home. But we certainly do meet under strange circumstances. What on earth led you into this business?"

"Thrift, thrift, Hugh," answered Walter, with a smile. "Let me tell you that I am making a good living and benefiting my fellow men."

"But it is such a change from Euclid College."

"True."

"Such a come down!"

"I don't know about that. I am afraid my career there was not particularly creditable. Now I am working and earning my own living. Can you wait till we get through here? Then I will talk with you as long as you like."

"Agreed. I am curious to hear of your adventures." Professor Robinson proposed to stay in Glenwood overnight, so that Walter had plenty of time to see his friend.

"My sister is to have a party of friends this evening, and she commissions me to invite you."

"But," hesitated Walter, "I have no dress suit here."

"You look well enough."

"Besides, I am filling a very humble position."

"We know who you are, and that you are a gentleman. That is enough. Will you come?"

"Yes, I will," answered Walter, heartily. "It will be like a taste of the old life."

"And if we should ask you to favor us on the violin?"

"I shall be glad to contribute to the pleasure of the evening. But you haven't told me why you are not back at college."

"My father is anxious to have me help him in his business. His health is not what it was. Not being likely to set the river on fire in any literary profession, I decided to give up the college for the counting-room."

"I think you did right."

CHAPTER XXI

MISS LONGWOOD'S PARTY

At eight o'clock Walter reached the Longwood mansion. It would have been early for a party in the city, but Glenwood people were sensible, and, beginning early, were able to close in good season.

The house was a handsome one, and the rooms, tastefully furnished, were blazing with light, and already half full.

Walter was quite at home in society, and advancing, greeted Hugh and his sister, by whom he was cordially received, and introduced to other members of the family.

About nine o'clock dancing commenced. Walter did not think it out of place to ask the hand of Laura Longwood, being so intimate with her brother. She had just accepted his invitation to dance, when a dark-complexioned young man, dressed in the extreme of the fashion, and evidently possessing a very high opinion of his appearance and position, approached, and with a ceremonious bow said: "Miss Longwood, may I have the pleasure of dancing with you?"

"Not this time, Mr. Murdock," answered the young

lady. "I am engaged to Mr. Sherwood."

Murdock upon this turned his glance upon Walter, whose dress, it must be confessed, was scarcely befitting the occasion, but it will readily be understood that he could not carry a dress suit about with him.

"Oh!" said Murdock, and his scornful glance spoke volumes.

"Let me introduce you to Mr. Sherwood, my brother's friend," continued the young lady.

"I am indeed honored by the introduction," said Murdock, bowing very low.

Walter colored, for it was evident that the tone was ironical. He bowed coldly, but did not speak.

The music struck up, and the dancing began. Though Walter was plainly dressed, he was a good dancer, and Miss Longwood had no occasion to be ashamed of her partner.

Murdock approached Hugh Longwood, who was busy in forming sets and was not dancing.

"Who is that dancing with your sister?" he asked abruptly.

"A college friend of mine - Walter Sherwood."

"He looks poor."

"I believe he has met with a reverse of fortune."

Horatio Alger, Jr.

"His face looks familiar. I am quite sure I have seen him somewhere."

"He only arrived in town to-day."

"I have it! He was playing the violin for a faker on the town common this afternoon."

"Yes; it was there I met him."

"Good heavens! and you invited him to your party?"

"Why not?" demanded Hugh coldly.

"The assistant and companion of a wandering faker!"

"No, Mr. Murdock, I did not invite him, for my sister saved me the trouble."

"I don't see how you could sanction her doing it."

"It strikes me, Murdock, you are interfering beyond your province. Walter Sherwood, you will be good enough to remember, is a gentleman by birth and education, and a college classmate of mine."

"That may all be, but think of his position!"

"Suppose we drop this discussion," said Hugh frigidly. "I shall invite whom I please, and shall ask advice of no one."

"Oh, if you take it that way, I will be silent."

"It will be as well."

The dance was over, and Murdock, approaching Miss Longwood once more, asked her hand for the next dance. She accepted, and they took their places on the floor.

"I can hardly expect to equal your last partner," said Murdock, in an ill-tempered tone.

Laura Longwood looked at him for a moment without speaking. She was ashamed of his ill breeding.

"Perhaps not," she answered composedly. "Mr. Sherwood is a very good dancer."

"I did not refer to that. I referred rather to his social position."

"He is of good family, I believe, but you need not be too modest as regards yourself."

"You overwhelm me," returned Murdock, with an exaggerated bow; "and you really think me the equal of Mr. Sherwood?"

"Is it necessary to discuss this question?" asked Laura, becoming more and more disgusted with her partner.

"I think I saw the gentleman this afternoon playing the violin on the wagon of a traveling faker."

"Yes, I saw him also."

"It is an excellent position for a young man - of family!" continued Murdock, with a scornful curl of the lip.

"Suppose we change the subject, Mr. Murdock," said Laura Longwood, with dignity. "If you desire a similar position you can speak to Mr. Sherwood."

"You are really very - very amusing, Miss Longwood," said Murdock, biting his lip. "I really don't aspire to such prominence. Besides, I don't play on the violin."

"That is a pity. It is a very fine instrument."

When the dance was concluded Murdock sought another, but was rather curtly refused. His efforts to injure Walter had only led to his own discomfiture. When, a little later, he saw Walter a second time dancing with Miss Longwood, he began to hate him.

During the last hour Walter obligingly consented to play on his favorite instrument, and his performance gave pleasure to the entire company, Murdock alone excepted.

When the party broke up, it chanced that Murdock and Walter took leave at the same time. Walter was slightly in advance when Murdock, quickening his pace, came up with him.

"Mr. Sherwood, I believe," he said.

"Yes, sir," answered Walter. "I believe I am addressing Mr. Murdock."

"You are. I hope you will pardon my giving you a little kindly advice."

"I certainly will if it is friendly," answered Walter.

"Then, don't you think you were a little out of place this evening?"

"What do you mean?" asked Walter quickly. "Where was I out of place?"

"At Miss Longwood's party."

"Why should I be? She invited me."

"No doubt."

"As her brother's friend and classmate."

"That is all very well, but you don't seem to consider your present position."

"Will you be good enough to tell me what is my present position?"

"You know better than I can tell you. You are the assistant of a low faker."

"I accompany Professor Robinson as a musical assistant, if that is what you mean."

"Professor Robinson!" repeated Murdock scornfully. "Where did he get his title?"

"You will have to ask him," said Walter, smiling.

"That is not the point, however. You are in his employ?"

"Well?"

"And yet you attend an evening party given by a young lady of high social position."

"Mr. Murdock, you may be surprised to learn that it is by no means the first social party of the kind that I have attended."

"That was before you became a faker."

"You will oblige me by not calling me a faker. I am earning my living honestly. I don't know your business."

"I am a lawyer," said Murdock haughtily.

"I wish you success in your chosen profession."

"You are truly kind!" said Murdock, in an unpleasant tone.

Walter looked at him gravely.

"Mr. Murdock," he said, "you have volunteered to give me advice."

"Which you are not inclined to take."

"Because I consider you officious in offering it. Now let me give you some advice."

"I shall be grateful, I am sure."

"Then let me advise you hereafter to mind your own business!"

"You are impertinent!" said Murdock angrily.

"That is my opinion of you. One thing more; you are quite at liberty to advise Miss Longwood not to take any notice of me."

"I shall do so."

"And you may be sure that I shall not call upon her without an invitation. It is hardly necessary to say this, as I leave town to-morrow, and it may be a long time before I visit Glenwood again."

Murdock heard this with satisfaction, for Walter's good looks and the evident favor with which he was regarded by Laura Longwood had made him jealous. He could not help, however, launching a final sarcasm.

"Don't think me unkind, my good fellow!" he said patronizingly. "I feel kindly disposed and as a proof will ask you to send round a bottle of your balm to my office. Shall I pay for it in advance?"

"No. I will mention your request to the professor, and he will probably be glad to furnish you with his medicine. Goodnight!"

They had reached the hotel, and Walter entered.

"That fellow is a snob," he said to himself. "He wishes me to feel that one in my position cannot be a gentleman. If he is one, I don't want to be. All his sneers won't make me ashamed of earning my living by an honest use of any gift that God has given me."

CHAPTER XXII

AN ADVENTURE

Three months passed without any incident worth recording. Professor Robinson's success was variable, but upon the whole he had reason to feel encouraged. He was an excellent salesman, and his balm, though it could not perform all the wonderful cures claimed for it, really had merit, and this helped materially.

So far as Walter was concerned, he found the professor an indulgent and honorable employer, whose word was as good as his bond. Every Saturday night there was a statement of sales for the week, and Walter was paid his commission of ten per cent. Though he was obliged to make some disbursements, the largest being for a suit of clothes, he found himself, at the end of fourteen weeks, possessed of a balance of a hundred dollars. This was a source of great satisfaction to Walter, who had known in Chicago how inconvenient it was to be without money.

One day the professor found himself in a Minnesota village. He had secured a vacant lot on the principal street for the display of his merchandise. He met with rather unusual success, a local celebration having drawn a considerable crowd to the town of Warwick. Walter, after playing on the violin, passed among the crowd with a supply of bottles of balm, while the professor was expatiating in an eloquent manner upon its merits. Among the crowd his attention was drawn to a roughly dressed man, in hunting costume, wearing a sombrero with a broad brim. His face was dark and his expression sinister. His eyes were very black and keen. He looked like a Spaniard, and the thought came to Waiter that he would make an ideal highway-man. He was leaning carelessly against the fence that separated the lot from the street. As Walter approached he moved slightly and accosted him.

"Say, young feller, is it all true that he" - with a jerk of his hand toward the professor - "says about this balm?"

"Yes, sir," answered Walter, in a business-like tone. "It is a very valuable remedy in all cases of bruise, sprain, rheumatism, headache, and other kindred troubles. Can I sell you a bottle?"

"Well, I don't mind," and the stranger drew out a silver quarter and tendered it in payment.

"Do you sell much of this stuff?" he asked carelessly.

"Yes, we have large sales."

"You are making money fast, I reckon?"

"We are doing very well," answered Walter, cautiously.

"It's an easy life to lead."

"Not so very easy. We are on the road early and late."

"Do you stop here overnight?"

"No; I think we will push on to Fremont."

"You'll get there late."

"Perhaps so. We shall not commence our sales till to-morrow.

"Why is he so inquisitive?" thought Walter, and as he turned back to scan once more the face of his recent customer he became more and more distrustful of him.

"Does that man live in town?" he inquired of a boy.

"Who? That man leaning against the fence?"

"Yes."

The boy shook his head.

"I never saw him before," he said. "I guess he came to the celebration."

When the sale was over Walter and the professor went to the hotel for supper. Walter caught sight of the mysterious stranger in the barroom, and could not avoid seeing that he himself was an object of attention. Why this should be he did not understand. If only he were a mind-reader and could interpret the man's thoughts it would have relieved his anxiety, for in spite of himself he was becoming anxious and apprehensive, though he could not explain why.

At supper the stranger sat opposite him. He ate heartily and with great rapidity, yet found time to glance repeatedly at Walter and his employer, as if he felt an interest in them.

Walter sought the professor after supper and communicated to him his fears.

Professor Robinson shrugged his shoulders.

"Your imagination is running away with you," he said. "I don't see anything extraordinary about this stranger, except that he is far from good-looking."

"Don't you think he has a sinister look?"

"He is as homely as the ace of spades, if that is what you mean. Suppose he is. All homely men are not suspicious characters. If they were, how would we be judged?" and the professor laughed in a jolly way.

"You have quite decided to go through to Fremont this evening?"

"Yes; I want to reach Stillman on Saturday - there is to be a county fair there - and to make it in time we must be moving to-night."

Of course, there was no more to be said. Walter did not care to interfere with the professor's plans, and he was ashamed to admit that he was nervous and alarmed. Perhaps his fears were groundless. He began to think so when at seven o'clock the stable-boy brought round a powerful black horse to the front of the inn, and the stranger who had given him so much anxiety vaulted into the saddle and rode away, without even turning to look at him.

Horatio Alger, Jr.

"Who is that fellow?" he asked of an old man who stood near, smoking a clay pipe.

The old man looked thoughtfully at the stranger, who had now ridden out of the yard.

"Seems to me I've seen that face before," he said slowly, "but I can't rightly tell where."

"He doesn't look like a farmer."

"No. If he lived anywhere within twenty miles I'd know him. He's a stranger."

"His looks don't recommend him."

"You're right there, boy."

"I shouldn't be surprised to hear that he was an outlaw."

"One of Jesse James' band, mayhap," suggested the old man, with a smile.

"Yes, he looks it."

"Well, he's gone, so he won't trouble us."

This was a consoling thought to Walter. He carried a hundred dollars in his pocket, and he had worked too hard for it to feel reconciled to its loss. The stranger, judging from his appearance, was quite capable of relieving him of it; but now he had ridden away, doubtless on business of his own, and the chances were that they would never meet again.

About eight o'clock Professor Robinson's team was brought round to the door, and he and Walter clambered upon the seat and were under way.

"Were you ever robbed, professor?" asked Walter.

The professor smiled.

"Yes," he said.

"By a highwayman?"

"No, by my assistant, a young man who occupied your place. He had been with me four weeks, and I reposed a good deal of confidence in him, as I do in you."

"I hope you won't repent your confidence in me, professor."

"I am sure I shall not. But to come back to my story, Charles Wright was a good-looking, smooth-faced fellow of twenty, and had a good turn for business. The trouble with him was that he was extravagant and never had a cent ahead."

"Did he earn as much as I do?"

"Yes, for business with me was unusually good at the time he was with me. However, he never could save money. Usually we occupied different rooms at the hotels we stopped at, but one night the hotel was crowded and we were obliged to room together. Now, as you know, I am a sound sleeper. I am asleep five minutes after my head touches the pillow, and even a thunder-storm during the night would scarcely waken me. On some accounts this is an advantage, but, as you will see, it turned out unluckily for me on the night I am speaking of. I awoke at the usual time - seven o'clock - and on opening my eyes I saw at once that my young assistant was not in the room. This gave me no uneasiness. I presumed that he had waked after a good night's sleep and was taking a morning walk. I rose from the bed, put on my clothes leisurely, and it was only after I was completely dressed that I felt in my pocket for my wallet. Then I made a startling discovery. The wallet was gone!"

"Was there much money in it?"

"About a hundred and ten dollars. Fortunately I had about fifty dollars, besides, in another pocket, so that I was not left quite penniless."

"Was your assistant the thief?"

"There is no doubt about it. He had gone downstairs at five o'clock, told the clerk he was going for a walk, and did not show up after that."

"Have you seen or heard of him since?"

"No; I may meet him again some time, but I doubt if I should have him arrested. He injured himself more than he did me. I lost a hundred dollars or more, but he lost a good place and his character for honesty. Depend upon it, Walter, honesty is the best policy in the long run."

"I am sure of that, sir."

Four miles from the hotel they entered a wood, through which the road ran for half a mile. It was dark, but not completely dark. A few stars sent down a faint light. By the light of these stars Walter descried a man, mounted on a large horse, stationed motionless in the middle of the road, apparently waiting for them to come up.

"Professor," he exclaimed, clutching his employer by the arm, "that's the man we saw at the hotel."

Horatio Alger, Jr.

CHAPTER XXIII

WALTER AND THE HIGHWAYMAN

The professor was startled at the exclamation, but was unwilling to believe that the man before him was a highwayman.

"My friend," he said, "won't you move to one side? You are in my path."

"We have a little business together," said the horseman, grimly, as he drew out and presented a revolver, "that must be attended to first."

"Do you wish a bottle of balm?" inquired Professor Robinson, in a tremulous voice.

"No; you may need one yourself unless we come to terms."

"What do you mean?"

"Hand over your pocketbook, old man, and be quick about it."

"I presume you are joking," said the professor nervously.

"You won't find it much of a joke!"

"Are you a - highwayman?" gasped the professor.

The other gave a quick, short laugh.

"You may call me that if you like," he said.

Now, Professor Robinson had, as was natural, a decided objection to surrendering his money, and, though there seemed little chance of producing an effect on the mind of the outlaw, ventured to remonstrate.

"My friend," he said, "if you are in want, I will lend, nay, give you five dollars, out of a spirit of humanity; but I trust you will not jeopardize your liberty by descending to robbery."

"Five dollars won't do, old man! Hand over your wallet, with all there is in it, and dry up that Sunday-school talk."

"What shall I do, Walter?" asked the poor professor.

"I am afraid you will have to let him have it, professor."

"That's where your head is level, boy!" said the highwayman approvingly. "Just fling over your wallet, and be quick about it."

"Tell him to ride up and get it," said Walter, in an undertone.

Though the professor did not understand Walter's

object in suggesting this, he was in a mood to be guided by any one, and repeated Walter's words.

"Anything to oblige," said the stranger.

"Don't give it to him till I say the word," whispered Walter.

The highwayman, lowering his revolver, rode up alongside of the wagon and held out his hand for the wallet.

Walter had conceived a bold scheme for disarming him and rendering him harmless.

"Give the wallet to me, professor," he said.

His employer meekly obeyed.

Then Walter, rising, dropped the wallet on the floor of the wagon, and reaching over suddenly grasped the revolver from the unsuspecting robber, and before he recovered from his amazement brought down the whip with terrible force on the flanks of his horse. The startled animal gave a spring that nearly unseated his rider and dashed madly down the road.

The robber was furious. As soon as he could he regained control of his steed and galloped back.

"Give me that revolver!" he shouted, in a rage.

Walter held the weapon in his hand and steadily pointed it at its late owner.

"I'll give you the contents if you don't ride off."

"Confound you, you young rascal! If you don't give me back my weapon I'll kill you!"

It was an empty threat, as Walter well knew.

"Do you hear me?" he said quietly.

The robber scanned him curiously. He had thought him a mere boy, without spirit or courage. Now he was compelled to revise his opinion of him. Threats would not answer. He must have recourse to strategy.

"You're smart, youngster. I'll give you credit for that," he said, in a milder tone. "You've got the best of me, I admit."

"Yes," answered Walter, "I have the advantage of you."

"I meant to take your money, but I won't do it now."

"Thank you!" said Walter, with an ironical smile.

"Just give me back that weapon of mine, and I'll ride off and let you alone."

"I don't think it would be wise."

The highwayman frowned.

"Don't be a fool, youngster!" he said. "Do you doubt my word?"

"I don't know you well enough to decide whether you are to be trusted, but I guess I'll keep the revolver."

"Then you will have robbed me."

"Walter," said the professor nervously, "perhaps you had better give him back his weapon. He has promised not to molest us further."

"That's where you talk sense, old man," said the robber approvingly. "You're a gentleman, you are."

"You hear, Walter?"

"Yes, youngster, you hear? Give me back my weapon and we'll part friends."

"And I trust, my friend, you will see the error of your ways and adopt some honest business."

"I will, old man, believe me!" said the robber, in a melodramatic tone. "I was not always thus."

"You will have my best wishes for your prosperity, and if you are in need I will give you five dollars."

"No, I will not take advantage of your liberal offer. Only give me the revolver and I will ride away."

"Come, Walter, give the man his revolver."

"Professor," said Walter, quietly, "you must excuse me, I can't comply with your request. This man is humbugging you. If I give him back the revolver you will have to give him your wallet too."

"Didn't I promise to ride away?" demanded the outlaw, angrily.

"Yes; but I have no confidence in your promise. Now, go at once, or I fire!"

Walter pointed the revolver full at the robber's head. He met the unflinching gaze of Walter's resolute eyes and saw that our hero was in earnest.

"Do you mean to keep my property?" he demanded hoarsely.

"No; come round to the hotel in Fremont to-morrow morning and you shall have your weapon."

With an execration the outlaw turned his horse and dashed off at full speed.

"There, he is gone!" said Walter, sinking back in his seat with an air of relief. His nerves had been at high tension, though he was outwardly calm, for he knew that he had to deal with a desperate man, and feared a sudden attack, which might have resulted disastrously for him.

"I don't know whether you have done right, Walter," said the professor, in a tone of mild deprecation.

"Surely, professor, you would not have had me give back the revolver?"

"He promised to ride off and leave us to ourselves."

"What is the word of such a man worth? He would have ridden off, but he would have carried with him your wallet and mine. Was there much money in yours?"

"Two hundred and fifty dollars."

"That's too much to lose. Take my advice, professor, and put the greater part of the money in one of your pockets. That is what I have done, for I suspected that this gentleman would lie in wait for us."

"What put it into your head to seize the pistol, Walter? If your attempt had miscarried he might have shot you."

"I don't propose to give up my money without a struggle. When the time came to act I moved suddenly upon the enemy. I did not propose to fail."

"You were very quick. You were like a flash of lightning."

"I meant to be," said Walter, smiling. "I haven't attended a gymnasium for nothing."

"Do you think he will attack us again?" asked the professor timidly.

"No; he has no revolver and I have. Besides, I don't mean to be taken at a disadvantage. If yon will drive, I will hold the revolver ready for instant use."

There was no further interruption during their ride, and about ten o'clock they drew up in front of the hotel in Fremont. Rooms were secured, and both Walter and the professor retired to rest.

About seven o'clock the next morning there was a knock at Walter's door. He opened it, half dressed, and found a boy of sixteen with a note in his hand.

"A gentleman gave me this for you," he said.

Walter opened the note and read these lines, which had been hastily scribbled:

"Give the bearer my revolver. I have a long journey before me and shall need it.

"YOU KNOW WHO."

"Where is the gentleman who gave you the note?" asked Walter.

"Down the road a piece. He asked me to be quick."

"Tell him," said Walter, putting the note in his vest pocket, "that he will have to come here himself."

He finished his toilet and went down to breakfast, but the robber did not put in an appearance. He probably thought that Walter was laying a trap for him.

Horatio Alger, Jr.

CHAPTER XXIV

AN ATTEMPT TO RECOVER THE REVOLVER

As Walter had been brought up with a strict sense of honesty, he was somewhat in doubt whether he ought to keep the revolver, which was a handsome one, silver-mounted. He decided, however, that it would be quixotic to disarm himself and put the outlaw in a position to renew his attack, as he undoubtedly would, if only because he would wish to get even with the boy who had humiliated him. Walter had, to be sure, promised to give it up if the owner called for it, but he meant at the same time to secure his arrest.

He did not mention to the professor that he had received a letter from the owner of the weapon, as his employer would have insisted upon his giving it up. Professor Robinson was a timid man, and, though he was of stout build and possessed a fair measure of strength, he had not as much spirit as some boys of ten.

"What are you going to do with the revolver, Walter?" he asked uneasily, as they set out on their way from Fremont to Stilwell.

"I am going to carry it with me, professor."

"Then you had better withdraw the charges."

"Why should I?"

"The weapon might go off."

"I mean that it shall if the owner makes another attack upon us."

"You don't think he will?" asked the professor, nervously.

"I think it very probable."

"I wish we had never met him," said the unhappy professor.

"So do I; but as we have, we must make the best of it."

"If you had only given him back the revolver we should have had no more trouble."

"Pardon me, professor, I think we should have had a great deal of trouble. Once give the fellow his old advantage over us and he would use it."

"I never had such an experience before," complained the professor, looking at Walter reproachfully, as if he thought that somehow it was the fault of his young assistant.

Walter smiled.

"Do you know, professor," he said, "your remark reminds me of a statement in an Irish paper to this effect: 'Several persons have died during the last year who never died before.'"

"I don't see the point," said the professor, peevishly.

They were about half-way to the next town when Walter heard the sound of a galloping horse behind him.

Looking out of the side of the wagon, he saw the now familiar figure of the outlaw as he rode up alongside. He looked critically at Walter, and saw that the coveted revolver was in our hero's hand, ready for action.

"Why didn't you give the revolver to my messenger this morning, boy?" he demanded, with a frown.

"I didn't think it would be safe," Walter answered significantly.

"Didn't you know it was my property?"

"I wasn't sure of it."

"What do you mean by that?"

"I didn't know whether you had paid for it."

"You are impudent. Professor Robinson, will you make the boy give me back my revolver?"

"I have told him to," answered the professor, in an apologetic tone, "but he won't obey me."

"Then why don't you discharge him? I wouldn't keep a boy in my employ who disobeyed me."

"I am well satisfied with him, except on this point."

"I am ready to leave you, professor, if you say the word," said Walter, and he made a motion as if to jump out of the wagon.

"No, no!" exclaimed the professor, in alarm. "I don't want you to leave me."

"Then I won't. I think it might be bad for you if I did," said Walter, with a significant look at the horseman.

"Well, boy," said the outlaw, harshly, "I can't waste my time here. You sent me a message to come for my revolver myself if I wanted it."

"Yes."

"Well, here I am. Now give me the weapon."

"I think I shall have to decline."

"Are you going back on your word?" demanded the outlaw.

"Not exactly."

"Then what do you propose to do?"

"Keep along with us till we reach Stilwell. Then we will go before a magistrate. You will make your demand for the weapon, and in his presence I will surrender it."

"Do you take me for a fool?" thundered the robber.

"No, and I want you to understand that I am not a fool, either."

"You are acting like a fool and a knave."

"I should certainly be acting like a fool if I gave up the revolver, and had it immediately pointed at me or my companion, with a demand for our money."

"But I gave you my word -"

"Of course you did, but I put no confidence in your word."

While this conversation was going on the poor professor looked on and listened with an expression of helplessness on his broad face. He was essentially a man of peace, and was by no means fitted to deal with a highwayman.

"Look here," said the outlaw, after a pause, and in a milder tone, "I have a special attachment for that weapon, or I would drop the whole matter and buy another one. But this was given me by an old pal, now dead, and I set great store by it. Professor, although the revolver is mine by rights, I will waive all that and offer you twenty-five dollars for it. That will pay you for all the trouble I have put you to."

Professor Robinson, though not a mean man, was fond of money, and this offer tempted him. It would be getting twenty-five dollars for nothing, and that was a piece of good luck not likely to present itself every day.

"I accept your offer," he said gladly.

"But I don't," put in Walter, calmly. "Allow me to say that the professor has no claim to the weapon. I took it with my own hand, and it has never been in his possession."

"All right! Then I'll give you twenty-five dollars for it."

"I decline your offer."

"I'd like to wring your neck, you young thief!"

"I have no doubt you would."

"Once more, and for the last time, will you give me back that revolver?"

"I have told you when and on what conditions I would surrender it."

"When?"

"At Stilwell, in the presence of a magistrate."

"You are very crafty. You want me to be arrested for attempted robbery."

"Yes, that is my wish."

"I've a great mind to snatch the revolver from you."

"Come on, then!" said Walter, holding it firmly, pointing at the outlaw.

"You've got the drop on me, youngster, but mark my word, I'll have that weapon yet, and I'll punish you for giving me all this trouble."

"Have you anything more to say?"

"No."

"Then suppose you ride on. We have been delayed long enough."

The robber did go, but aimed a volley of imprecations at Walter, of which the latter took no notice.

In the early evening they arrived at Stilwell and secured rooms at the hotel.

Among the guests was a cattleman from Dakota, who had been to Chicago with a herd of cattle and was now on his way back. He was loud in his complaints of a highwayman whom he had met two days previous, who had relieved him of a wallet containing five hundred dollars.

"Won't you describe him?" asked Walter, struck by a sudden suspicion.

The cattle dealer did so. His description tallied with the personal appearance of Walter's enemy.

"Was he on foot?" asked Walter.

"No; he was on a black horse."

Walter nodded.

"I know him," he said.

"Has he robbed you?"

"No; I have robbed him."

"What do you mean?" inquired the cattle dealer, in wonder.

"Do you recognize this?" and Walter exhibited the revolver.

"Yes; it looks like the revolver he pointed at me."

"Probably it is."

"But how do you happen to have it?"

"I took it from him."

"You - a mere boy!" exclaimed the cattle dealer, incredulously.

"Yes. I will tell you about it."

And Walter gave an account of the circumstances under which the revolver had come into his possession.

"It is a handsome weapon," said the cattle dealer, taking it into his hands and examining it. "It must be worth a hundred dollars."

"I think I shall keep it for my own use," said Walter, quietly.

"I'll give you seventy-five dollars for it."

"I would rather not part with it. Indeed, I should not feel justified in selling it, considering the way it came into my hands."

"Well, boy, you're a smart one; but I surmise you haven't seen the last of the owner."

The speaker was right.

CHAPTER XXV

DICK RANNEY'S SCHEME

Dick Ranney - for the first time we give the name of the highwayman - had no intention of going away without his revolver. It had been his constant companion for years, and had served him well during his connection with the famous band of Jesse James. Now, his leader dead, he was preying upon the community on his own account. So daring and so full of resources was he that he had never been arrested but once, and then managed to escape from the cabin in which he was temporarily confined.

The weapon he was so anxious to recover had been given him by his old commander, and for this reason, and also because the revolver was a very handsome and valuable one, he was willing to expose himself to the risk of capture in order to recover it.

The opposition he met with from a "beardless boy" - as he styled Walter - irritated and surprised him. He was fifty pounds heavier than Walter, and he had expected that a mere boy would give in almost immediately. But he saw that he had misjudged the lad. He was little more than a boy in years and appearance, but he evidently had a man's courage and spirit. Ranney would have secured another revolver if he had not felt

Horatio Alger, Jr.

so certain of recovering his own. After his last failure he began to consider what course to adopt.

It was easy to find out the professor's route. He knew that he was to stay a night at Stilwell, and to Stilwell he went. He did not venture into the village until nightfall, and then, for reasons easy to divine, he abstained from visiting the hotel.

Looking about for a confederate, his attention was drawn to a boy of sixteen who was sawing wood in front of a humble cottage half a mile from the village.

"I see you know how to work," said Dick Ranney, affably, as he leaned carelessly against the fence.

"I know how, but I don't like it," answered the boy, pausing in his task.

"I don't blame you. I don't like that kind of work myself."

"I guess you don't have to do it now," answered the boy, glancing at the neat and expensive attire of his new acquaintance.

"Well, no; I can do better."

"Are you in business?"

"Yes," answered Ranney, vaguely. "I am traveling for a house in New York."

"I should like that."

"Give me your name. I may be able to give you a place

some day."

"My name is Oren Trott."

Dick Ranney took out a note-book and put the name down, greatly to the boy's satisfaction.

"By the way," went on Ranney, "do you want to earn half a dollar?"

"Yes," answered Oren, with alacrity.

"Perhaps I can put you in the way of doing so. Do you know the hotel people?"

"Yes, sir. I worked there for a short time."

"All the better. Then you know about the house, the location of rooms, etc.?"

"Yes, sir."

"There are two parties staying there in whom I am interested. One is Professor Robinson."

"Yes, I know - the man that sells bottles of balm."

"The same."

"I saw him come into town with his wagon."

"Well, I want to find what room he will occupy to-night. The fact is," he continued, as he noted Oren's look of surprise, "the man owes me quite a sum of money and is trying to evade payment."

Horatio Alger, Jr.

"He doesn't look like that kind of man," said Oren, thoughtfully.

"My boy, you are young and are hardly qualified to judge of a man by his appearance. The man looks honest, I admit, but he's slippery. And, by the way, did you notice a young fellow in the wagon with him?"

"Yes, sir; he isn't much larger than I am."

"Exactly so. Well, I want to find out what room he occupies, also."

"Yes, sir," answered Oren, looking a little surprised.

"You see," explained Dick Ranney, "I want to make the professor a call, and I can perhaps tell from the outside whether he is in or not. He will avoid meeting me if he can. Now, do you think you can find out for me what I require?"

"Yes, sir."

"Then go at once."

"Shall I find you here when I get back?" asked Oren, cautiously.

"Yes."

"I wouldn't like to take all that trouble for nothing."

"You won't. Here is a quarter in advance, and I will give you the fifty cents besides if you find out what I wish."

"Good for you! You're a gentleman!" said Oren, with an expression of satisfaction on his honest country face.

Two hours later Walter and the cattle dealer returned from a walk they had taken together. Walter found his new acquaintance, though not an educated man, an agreeable companion, and by no means deficient in shrewdness, though he had allowed himself to be robbed by Dick Ranney.

They went up to the desk for their keys.

"Will you two gentlemen do me a favor?" asked the clerk.

"What is it?" asked the cattle dealer.

"A gentleman and lady have just arrived and want to stay here to-night, but the number of our rooms is limited and we are full. Now, if you, sir, will go into Mr. Sherwood's room - there are two beds there - we shall be able to give the party yours."

"I have no objection if he hasn't," said the cattle dealer.

"I have none whatever," said Walter, cheerfully.

"Then we can fix it. I am sure I am very much obliged to you both. By the way, Mr. Sherwood, there was a boy here a little while since who was anxious to find out what room you occupied, also what room was Professor Robinson's."

"A boy?" repeated Walter, puzzled.

Horatio Alger, Jr.

"Yes, a village boy - Oren Trott."

"I don't know any such boy."

"He is a good, industrious lad."

"That may all be, but what does he want to know about my room for?"

"That's the question I put to him. I found him very close-mouthed at first, but finally he admitted that he was employed by some man - a stranger in the village - to find out."

Walter and the cattle dealer exchanged glances. The same thought had come to each.

"Did he describe the man?"

"No; it seems he did not take much notice of him."

"Was that all the boy wanted to know?"

"Yes."

"He didn't say what the man's object was in seeking this information?"

"No. Probably he didn't know."

Walter and his new friend, whom we will call Manning, went upstairs.

"What does it all mean, Mr. Manning?" asked Walter.

"It probably means that our old friend proposes to

make a call upon you during the night."

"Do you really think so?" asked Walter, naturally startled at the suggestion.

"Yes. You still have his revolver, you know."

"I think he will find me ready for him," said Walter, resolutely.

"He will find us ready, you mean," corrected Manning. "You know I am going to be your roommate."

"I am glad of that, under the circumstances."

"So am I. I should like to recover the money the fellow robbed me of. I should like to know his name."

"I can tell you that. I was examining the revolver this afternoon, when I saw a name engraved upon it in very small letters."

"What name?"

"R. Ranney."

"Then," said Manning, in excitement, "he is the famous Dick Ranney, formerly with Jesse James."

"I never heard of him."

"He is well known in this Western country. Why, there is a reward of a thousand dollars offered for his apprehension."

"I should like to earn that money," said Walter.

"You shall; and this very night, if I can bring it about."

"Half of the reward should be yours."

"I am rich enough without It. As to the money the fellow robbed me of, I shall try to recover that, though the loss won't in the least embarrass me."

"How do you think Ranney will try to get into the room?"

"Through the window. The casements are loose, and nothing could be easier."

Walter went to the window and found that there was no way of fastening it.

"I think we could fasten it with a knife."

"I don't want it fastened," said Manning.

"Why not?"

"I want Mr. Ranney to get into the room. Once in, we must secure him. If we are smart, our enterprising visitor will find himself in a trap."

CHAPTER XXVI

THE EVENTS OF A NIGHT

In the country it may safely be assumed that by twelve o'clock at night every sound and healthy person will be asleep. Dick Ranney gave an extra margin of half an hour, and thirty minutes after midnight made his appearance in the hotel yard. Thanks to the information given by his young messenger, Oren Trott, who, of course, did not know that in this way he was assisting a dishonest scheme, he was able to fix at once upon the windows of the rooms occupied by Walter and the professor.

He decided to enter Walter's chamber first, partly because he wanted his revolver, which would be of service to him in case he were attacked. Then, again, he wanted the satisfaction of triumphing over the boy who had had the audacity to defy him - a full-grown man, and one whose name had carried terror to many a traveler.

There was a long ladder leaning against the stable. Dick Ranney could not call this providential without insinuating that Providence was fighting on the side of the transgressor, but he called it, appropriately, a "stroke of luck," as indeed it seemed at the time.

Horatio Alger, Jr.

He secured the ladder and put it up against the window of Walter's room. The window, as he could see, was partly open, it being a summer night.

Dick Ranney observed this with a grim smile of satisfaction.

"He's making things easy for me," he said to himself.

As softly and cautiously as a cat he ascended the ladder, but not softly enough to escape the vigilant ear of Manning, who was expecting him.

Manning at the sound stepped from the bed - he had thrown himself on the outside, without undressing - and stepped into a closet, as he did not wish Ranney to learn that there were two persons in the chamber. Walter was awake, but he lay in bed motionless and with his eyes closed. The revolver was in Manning's hands, but he had placed his clothing temptingly over a chair between the bed and the window, but in such a position that his companion on coming out of the closet would be between the window and the burglar. Dick Ranney stood on the ladder and looked in.

What he saw reassured him. Walter was in bed, and seemed to be fast asleep.

"The coast is clear," he murmured softly. "Now, where is the revolver?"

He could not see it, but this did not trouble him. Probably the boy had it under his pillow, and in that case he could obtain it without trouble. Meanwhile, it would be well to secure the boy's pocketbook. Though he underrated Walter's wealth, he thought he might have twenty dollars, and this would be worth taking.

He lifted the window softly and entered the room. In order to deaden the sound of his steps he had taken off his shoes and placed them on the ground beside the foot of the ladder.

Having entered the room, he strode softly to the chair over which Walter had thrown his clothes and began to feel in the pockets of his pantaloons. There was a purse in one of the pockets which contained a few small silver coins, but it is needless to say that Walter had disposed of his stock of bank bills elsewhere. He felt that prevention of robbery was better than the recovery of the goods stolen.

Meanwhile, Manning, whose hearing was keen, was made aware through it that the burglar had entered the room. He opened the door of the closet and, walking into the center of the apartment, placed himself, revolver in hand, in front of the window.

Though his motions were gentle, the outlaw's ears were quick. He turned swiftly, and with a look of dismay realized that he had walked into a trap. He had not felt afraid to encounter a boy of eighteen, but here was a resolute man, who had the advantage of being armed, and well armed.

Dick Ranney surveyed him for a minute in silence, but was very busily thinking what were his chances of escape.

"Well," said Manning, "we meet again!" "Again?" repeated Ranney, in a questioning tone.

Horatio Alger, Jr.

"Yes. When we last met, you had the drop on me and relieved me of my wallet. To-night I have the drop on you."

Dick Ranney paused for reflection.

"That's so," he said. "Do you want your wallet back?"

"Yes."

"Then we'll make a bargain. Give me that revolver, promise not to raise the house, and I will give you back your wallet."

"With all the money inside?"

"Yes."

"I don't think I will," said Manning, after a pause.

"Don't be a fool! Come, be quick, or the boy will wake up."

"He is awake already," said Walter, raising his head from the pillow.

"Were you awake when I entered the room?" asked Dick Ranney, quickly.

"Yes."

"Fooled again!" exclaimed Ranney, bitterly. "Boy, I believe you are my evil genius. Till I met you, I thought myself a match for any one."

"You were more than a match for me," said Manning,

"but he wins best who wins last."

"Well, what do you mean to do?" asked Ranney, doggedly.

"To capture you, Dick Ranney, and hand you over to the law which you have so persistently violated."

"That you will never do," said Ranney, and he dashed toward the window, thrusting Manning to one side.

But what he saw increased his dismay. The ladder had been removed, and if he would leave the room he must leap to the ground, a distance of over twenty feet.

"Confusion!" he exclaimed. "The ladder is gone!"

"Yes, I directed the stable-boy to keep awake and remove it," explained Manning.

"I may be taken, but I will be revenged first," shouted Dick Ranney, and he flung himself on Manning, who, unprepared for the sudden attack, sank to the floor, with Ranney on top. But the outlaw's triumph was short-lived. Walter sprang to Manning's rescue, seized the revolver, and, aiming it at the burglar, cried quickly:

"Get up, or I'll fire!"

Dick Ranney rose sullenly. He paid Walter the compliment of believing he meant what he said.

"It's your turn, boy," he muttered.

"Stay where you are!" ordered Walter, and he walked

slowly backward, still covering the robber with the revolver, till he reached the door opening into the entry.

Dick Ranney watched him closely, and did not offer any opposition, for it occurred to him that the opening of the door would afford him a better chance for flight.

No sooner, therefore, was the door open than he prepared to avail himself of the opportunity, running the risk of a bullet wound, when his plans were frustrated by the entrance of two village constables - strong, sturdy men.

"Dick Ranney, do you surrender?" asked Walter, in a clear, resolute tone.

Ranney looked slowly from one to the other and calculated the chances. The ladder was gone and he found himself facing four foes, three of them strong men, some of them armed.

"It's all up with me!" he said quietly. "I surrender."

"You do wisely," remarked Manning. "Now, will you restore my wallet?"

The outlaw took it out of his pocket and handed it over.

"There it is," he said. "I suppose you won't me to pay interest for the use of the money."

The two constables advanced, and one of them took out a pair of handcuffs.

"Hold out your hands!" he said.

The burglar did so. He saw that opposition would not benefit him, and he yielded to the inevitable with a good grace.

"It seems I walked into a trap," he said. "If you don't mind telling me, were you expecting me?"

"Yes," answered Walter.

"Did the boy betray me?" he asked quickly.

"No; the boy suspected nothing wrong, but his questions excited suspicion."

"Dick Ranney," said the outlaw, apostrophizing himself, "you're a fool! I should like to kick you!"

"I think you were imprudent, Mr. Ranney," said Manning,

"It was this revolver that undid me," said Ranney. "I wanted to recover it, for it was given me by my old captain. It was never out of my possession till that boy snatched it from me. I suppose it was to be," and he sighed, comforted, perhaps, by the thought that it would have been useless to struggle against fate.

CHAPTER XXVII

WALTER BECOMES A CAPITALIST

Professor Robinson slumbered on, blissfully unconscious of the events that had made the night an exciting one. When he came downstairs early in the morning he strayed accidentally into the room where Dick Ranney was confined under guard. Being short-sighted, he did not see the captive until Ranney hailed him.

"Good morning, professor!"

The professor skipped nimbly back and gazed at the prisoner in alarm.

"You here?" he exclaimed.

"Yes," answered Dick, grimly.

"But how did it happen?"

"I came to the hotel a little after midnight to make you a call, but went first to the room of your assistant."

"What, after midnight?"

"Yes. It is hardly necessary to explain what happened. Here I am!"

"Ah, my friend," said the professor, "this may be fortunate for you, if it leads you to consider and reflect upon the errors of your life."

"Oh, stow that!" exclaimed Ranney, in disgust. "I'm not that kind of a man. I follow my own course and take the consequences."

The professor shook his head sadly and went out. Later, when he heard what had happened, he said to Walter: "If that man had come into my room at midnight I should have died of fright."

"There was no occasion to be alarmed," returned Walter, "We were prepared for him."

"I - I am afraid I was never cut out for a hero," said the professor. "My nervous system is easily upset."

The plain truth was that Professor Robinson was a born coward, though he was stronger and more muscular, probably, than Grant, Sherman or Sheridan. But it is not brawn and muscle that make a hero, but the spirit that animates the man, and of this spirit the professor had very little. Yet in after years when he had retired from business and was at leisure to live over again his past life, he used to tell with thrilling effect how he and Walter had trapped and captured the daring outlaw, Dick Ranney, and received admiring compliments upon his courage and prowess, which he complacently accepted, though he knew how little he deserved them.

It so chanced that Stilwell was the county seat and court was in session at that time, and nearly ready to wind up its business. It was owing to this circumstance that the trial of Dick Ranney was held at once. By request Walter and the professor remained to bear testimony against the prisoner, and Manning also strengthened the case against him. Within less than a week the trial was concluded, a verdict of guilty was brought in, and the prisoner sentenced to a ten years' term of imprisonment.

Dick Ranney heard the sentence with philosophical calmness.

"My good friend," said the professor, "I trust that in your long years of confinement you will reflect upon -"

"Don't worry about that," interrupted Dick. "I sha'n't be in prison three months."

"But I thought -"

"Bolts and bars can be broken, professor. When I do get out I will inquire what part of the country you are in and will make you a visit."

This promise, so far from cheering Professor Robinson, seemed to disconcert him extremely, and he shortened his talk with his road acquaintance.

After the trial was over Walter was waited upon by an official, who tendered him the reward of one thousand dollars offered for the capture of Dick Ranney.

"Mr. Manning has waived his claim in your favor," explained the official, "and therefore there is no question that to you belongs the reward."

"There are two others whose services deserve recognition," said Walter; "the two constables who made the arrest."

"There is no additional sum at our command," explained the official.

"None is needed," returned Walter. "I shall pay each a hundred dollars out of the reward which has been awarded to me."

It is needless to say that the two constables, both of whom were poor men with large families, were very grateful for this substantial recognition of their services.

CHAPTER XXVIII

WALTER GOES OUT OF BUSINESS

By the time Walter received his prize of eight hundred dollars he had saved enough out of his wages to make nearly a thousand. He reflected with pride that this money had not been left him, but was the fruit of his own exertions. He resolved to say nothing in his letters home of his good fortune, but wait till he returned, when he would have the pleasure of taking his guardian by surprise.

A day later he received a letter from Doctor Mack, which had been forwarded from one place to another, and was now nearly three weeks old.

It ran thus:

DEAR WALTER: You give but scanty intelligence of your progress and success, or want of it. I respect you for your determination to support yourself, but I don't want you to carry your independence too far. As you have never fitted yourself for any kind of business, I presume your earnings are small. I should not be surprised to hear that you are straitened for money. If you are, don't let your pride prevent your informing me. I can easily send you fifty dollars, for your property was not all lost, and it is not fitting that you should deprive yourself of the comforts of life when there is no occasion for it.

"Nancy often speaks of you, and, indeed, I may say that we both miss you very much, and wish the year were up, so that you might return to us. I have hopes of righting your property, so that you may go back to Euclid College at the beginning of the fall session. I am glad to learn by your last letter that your health is excellent. Once more, don't hesitate to write to me for money if you need a remittance.

"Your affectionate guardian,

"EZEKIEL MACK."

Walter smiled as he finished reading the letter.

"I wonder what my good guardian would say," he soliloquized, "if he knew that I had nearly a thousand dollars saved up? He would open his eyes, I fancy."

He sat down at once and made a reply, in the course of which he said: "Don't trouble yourself to send me money. I can get along with the wages I receive. When I left home I made up my mind not to call upon you for help, and I am glad to say there is no occasion to do so as yet. I think my year's absence from college will do me good. I am ashamed when I consider how poorly I appreciated the advantages of study, and how foolishly I spent my time and money. If I ever go back to college I shall turn over a new leaf. I have seen something of the world and gained some experience of life, and feel about half a dozen years older than when I left college."

When Doctor Mack, a week later, read these lines he smiled contentedly.

"My experiment is working well," he said. "It is making a man of Walter. He has been a drone, hitherto. Now he has become a worker, and, though I may not like him better, for he was always near to my heart, I respect him more."

A week later Walter, on returning from a walk, found a middle-aged stranger in conversation with Professor Robinson.

The professor seemed a little embarrassed when Walter entered.

"I have some news for you, Walter," he said. "I am afraid it will not be welcome to you."

"Please let me hear it, professor," said Walter.

"This gentleman is Nahum Snodgrass, of Chicago, who has been for some years a traveler for a large wholesale-drug-house."

"I am glad to meet you, Mr. Snodgrass," said Walter, politely.

Snodgrass, who was a thin, dry-looking man, nodded briefly.

"I have just sold out my business to him," went on Professor Robinson, "and henceforth shall aim to live more easily and enjoy the presence of my family."

"I congratulate you, professor," said Walter. "I think

you deserve a life of leisure."

"Mr. Snodgrass is willing to take you into his employ, but he does not think he can afford to pay you as much as I did."

"No," said Snodgrass, clearing his throat, "I find that Professor Robinson has been foolishly liberal. The ten per cent. commission which he has paid you is simply - stu - pendous!"

Walter smiled.

"I have not been in the habit of taking that view of it," he said.

"Perhaps not, but I do," said Snodgrass, firmly. "You are a very young man, and ought not to expect much pay. I will give you two dollars a week and pay your traveling expenses."

"I beg to decline your offer, Mr. Snodgrass," said Walter, politely. "I have thought of changing my business before, but was unwilling to leave the professor. As we are strangers, I need have no further hesitation."

"Young man," said Snodgrass, "I think you are making a mistake. It will not be so easy getting another place as you suppose."

"Perhaps not, but I can afford to live a few weeks without work."

"Your savings will soon go" - Snodgrass knew nothing of Walter's prize money - "and then what will you do?"

"Trust to luck," answered Walter, lightly.

Nahum Snodgrass shook his head gloomily. He thought Walter a very foolish young man.

Had Walter lost his position two months earlier it would have been a serious matter to him, but now, with a capital of nearly a thousand dollars, he could afford to be independent. As he expressed it, he could afford to be idle for a few weeks. Still, he didn't wish to remain unemployed for a long time. He felt happier when at work, but wished to secure some employment that would be congenial.

"Mr. Snodgrass," said the professor, "I think you are making a mistake in not employing Walter Sherwood."

Nahum Snodgrass shrugged his shoulders.

"I don't mean to pay away all my profits to an assistant," he said.

"But you can't get along alone very well."

"I will try, unless I can find some one that will take what I am willing to pay."

He finally succeeded in doing this. A young man of eighteen, employed in a drug-store in town, who was on the point of being discharged, agreed to take the position, and stepped into Walter's place. To anticipate a little, he disappeared two weeks later, carrying with him fifty dollars belonging to his employer.

Walter stayed two days longer at the hotel, and then, sending his valise ahead to Burnton, twenty miles farther on, started to walk the distance. He was in a mountainous country, and the scenery was wild and attractive, so that he felt that this arrangement would prove agreeable to him. He provided himself with a stout staff and started at good speed. He had accomplished about eight miles, when he was overtaken by a shabbily dressed traveler riding on the back of a fine horse. The horseman slackened his pace when he reached Walter.

"Good morning, stranger!" he said.

"Good morning!" responded Walter, turning his head.

"I am glad to have company. It's a lonesome stretch of road here."

"Yes," answered Walter, carelessly. "But there isn't any danger, is there?"

"Well, there might be. A friend of mine was stabbed and robbed here three months since."

"Indeed!"

"Yes; and though I haven't much money with me, I shouldn't like to be robbed of what I have."

"It would be inconvenient."

"Do you carry much money with you?" asked the other, in a careless tone.

Walter was not disposed to take a stranger into his confidence.

"Not much!" he responded.

"You are prudent. Are you armed?"

Walter drew out Dick Ranney's revolver, which he still carried. The stranger eyed him respectfully.

"That's a mighty handsome weapon," he said. "Just let me look at it."

Walter began to think he had fallen in with a highwayman again.

CHAPTER XXIX

WALTER BUYS A HORSE

"You can look at the pistol as I hold it," said Walter, in response to the request recorded at the close of the preceding chapter.

"I say," remarked the stranger suddenly, "don't you want to buy a horse?"

"How much do you ask for the horse?" he inquired.

"I want to get her off my hands. Give me fifty dollars, and she's yours."

Walter had a pad in his satchel and a fountain pen in his pocket. He hastily wrote out the following form:

"In consideration of fifty dollars by me received, I give and transfer to Walter Sherwood my roan horse." Here followed a brief description of the animal.

"Now put your name there, and I will hand you the money," said Walter.

"Thank you, stranger! You've got a good bargain."

"I agree to that," said Walter.

Horatio Alger, Jr.

"I suppose the horse is sound?" he said inquiringly.

"Sound as a die! Don't you take no trouble about that. It goes to my heart to give her up. Good-by, old gal!"

Walter touched the horse lightly with his whip, and she bounded forward. After a few miles he reached a town of good size. Riding along the main street his attention was drawn to a printed notice in front of a store. It read thus:

"HORSE STOLEN!

"Stolen from the subscriber, on the evening of the twenty-fifth, a roan mare, eight years old and sixteen hands high, with a white mark between the eyes. Answers to the name of Bess. Whoever will return her to the subscriber, or give information that will lead to her recovery, will receive a suitable reward.

"COLONEL RICHARD OWEN, Shelby."

A terrible suspicion entered Walter's mind. He recognized the white mark. Then he called "Bess." The mare half turned her head and whinnied.

CHAPTER XXX

WALTER FINDS HIMSELF IN A TIGHT PLACE

Walter had hardly time to consider what to do in the light of the discovery he had made before the matter was taken out of his hands.

"Young feller, you'd better get off that hoss!" fell on his ears in a rough voice.

He turned, and saw two stalwart men eyeing him suspiciously.

"Gentlemen," said Walter earnestly, "till I read this notice I had no idea that the horse was stolen."

"That's neither here nor there. You'd better get off the hoss."

Walter felt that this was a command, and obeyed at once.

"Very well, gentlemen," he said. "I will leave the horse in your hands, and depend upon you to return it to the owner."

As Walter spoke he turned to walk off, but the man who had first accosted him got in his way.

Horatio Alger, Jr.

"I don't want to have any trouble with you, sir. Please get out of my way, and let me go."

"Not by a long shot."

"What do you propose to do with me?"

"Take you to the lockup."

Walter was now really alarmed.

"You'll have to go with us, young feller!" said Crane.

"And leave the hoss?" asked Penton. "We'd ought to take charge of it, and get the reward."

"That's so, Penton. You go and get a constable. We'll stand by the hoss."

Penton hurried off, and returned shortly with a constable in uniform.

"What's up?" he asked.

"This young feller's rid into town with Colonel Richard Owen's hoss."

"But I'd ought to secure the hoss," said the constable, who felt that perhaps he might be entitled to the reward offered.

"Look here, Cyrus Stokes, you secure the thief - that's your lookout."

"Gentlemen," said Walter, "I object to being called a thief. I have already told you I did not steal the horse."

The constable seized Walter by the arm and walked off with him. To add to his mortification, people whom they met on the street looked at him curiously.

Horatio Alger, Jr.

CHAPTER XXXI

IN THE LOCKUP

The lockup was a basement room under the engine-house. There were four cells, about four by eight, and into one of these Walter was put. The cell opposite was occupied by a drunken tramp, who looked up stupidly as Walter entered, and hiccoughed: "Glad to see you sonny."

"And I must stay in here overnight - with that man?"

"Hoss-stealers mustn't be particular," said the constable.

"Can you tell me where Colonel Owen lives - the man that owns the horse?"

"You ought to know that!"

"Is there any lawyer in this village?"

"Yes, there's two, an old man and a young one."

"I should like to see one of them. Can you ask one of them to come here?"

"It's a leetle out of my way," suggested

Constable Stokes.

The constable pocketed with alacrity the half-dollar our hero tendered him, and said briskly. "I'll send him right off."

"I shay," interjected the tramp, "send me a lawyer, too."

"The same man will do for you," replied the constable. "A lawyer won't do you no good, though."

"We're victims of tyrannical 'pression!" said the tramp gloomily. "What are you in for, young feller?"

"I'm charged with stealing a horse."

"Smart boy!" said the tramp admiringly. "I didn't think you was up to hoss-stealin'."

"I am not. The charge is false."

"That's right! Stick to it! Deny everything. That's what I do." Half an hour later the outer door was opened and the constable reappeared, followed by a young man of about thirty.

"This is Mr. Barry, the lawyer," he said. "Mr. Barry, here is the key. You can keep it and let yourself out if you will be responsible for the safe custody of the prisoner."

"Yes, Mr. Stokes, I will give you my word that he shall not escape. Which is my client?"

"You don't look like a criminal, certainly," said the

lawyer, with a rapid survey of his new client.

"I hope not."

"But one can't go by appearances wholly. As your lawyer, for I will undertake your case, I must ask you to trust me entirely, and give me your full confidence.

"First, let me ask your name."

"Walter Sherwood."

"It will now be necessary for you to tell me frankly whether you stole the horse or not."

"Of course I did not," answered Walter indignantly.

"You must excuse my asking the question. I did not believe you guilty, but it was necessary for me to know positively from your own lips. You must not be sensitive."

"I have no right to be, but I find myself in a very trying position."

"Of course, but I will try to get you out of it. Now, will you tell me in detail how the horse came into your possession?"

Walter told the story, and the lawyer listened attentively.

"Have you any proof of what you assert?" he asked, when Walter finished.

"There was no one present."

"I suppose not. Did no papers pass between you and this man?"

"Oh, yes!" answered Walter quickly, and he drew out the receipt which he had drawn up and got Hank Wilson to sign.

"Come, this is very important!" said Mr. Barry cheerfully. "It is a very valuable confirmation of your story. Will you trust me with it?"

"Certainly, sir."

"Is there any suggestion you have to offer, Mr. Sherwood? Sometimes I find that my clients give me valuable assistance that way."

"I wish you would telegraph to Colonel Owen to come here."

"Probably he has been sent for, but if not I will request him to come. Do you know the colonel?"

"No, sir; I never heard his name till I read the advertisement. Do you know anything of him, Mr. Barry?"

"He is the owner of a large estate in Shelby, and is a thorough gentleman of the old school."

"All the better! I would rather deal with such a man. Besides, by describing the man of whom I bought the horse I may put him in the way of capturing the real thief."

"Well thought of. May I ask, Mr. Sherwood, if you are

from this part of the country?"

"No; I am a native of New York State.

"A year ago I was a member of the sophomore class of Euclid College."

"That is strange!" ejaculated Barry. "What is strange?"

"Colonel Owen, the owner of the horse, is an old graduate of the same institution."

"Is it possible?" exclaimed Walter, in genuine amazement.

"It is quite true. I am glad to have made the discovery. It will prepossess him in your favor, and this, I need hardly say, will be a great point gained. Well, I believe I have obtained all the data I require, and I will now go home and think over your case. I wish I could take you with me."

"I wish you could; I hate to be left in such a place."

"Cheer up, Mr. Sherwood. It won't be for long, I predict. You may rest assured of my best efforts in your behalf. I will at once telegraph for Colonel Owen."

The evening glided wearily away. Walter threw himself on his pallet and was nearly asleep when a confused noise was heard outside, and heavy blows were rained upon the outer door.

"What does it mean?" asked Walter, bewildered.

He listened intently, and there came to his ears a shout which made him turn pale with terror.

CHAPTER XXXII

AN AWFUL MOMENT

"Bring out the hoss thief! Lynch him! Lynch him!"

"What's up?" asked the tramp drowsily, opening his eyes.

"Bring out the hoss thief!" cried a dozen rough voices, as the battering at the door was repeated.

"They want you, young feller!" he continued, as he caught the meaning of the cry.

"What shall we do?" asked Walter helplessly.

"They don't want me," returned the tramp complacently. "It's you they want!"

"You will stand by me?" implored Walter, eager for any help.

"Won't do no good! There's a crowd of them. You're in a bad box, young feller!"

"Have you got a pistol?"

"No."

Then it flashed upon Walter that he still had the revolver which belonged to Dick Ranney.

"I will sell my life dearly!" thought Walter, "They shan't kill me without some resistance."

"Open the door, or it'll be wuss for ye!" cried a rough voice.

The door was strong, but it did not long withstand the fierce attacks made upon it. Walter, by the light that came in through a crevice, saw it sway and gradually yield to the impetuous attacks of the mob.

"Here's the hoss thief!" exclaimed the leader, throwing the light into the cell occupied by the inebriate.

The tramp was alarmed and completely sobered by the terrible suggestion.

"I ain't the man!" he said. "It's that young feller yonder."

The man with the lantern turned in the direction of the other cell.

"He's only a kid!" he said doubtfully.

"All the same, he's the hoss thief!" said the tramp earnestly.

"Is he telling the truth?" asked the leader, turning to the men who were just behind him.

"He looks most like the hoss thief!" said Dan Muggins. "The other's a milk-and-water chap, just out of boardin'-school."

"You're right! Smash in the cage!"

CHAPTER XXXIII

WALTER SAVES ANOTHER'S LIFE

Meanwhile the feelings of Walter were hard to describe. He saw that perhaps his only chance of life lay in remaining quiet and letting the mistake remain uncorrected.

On the other hand, the poor wretch was as much entitled to life as he.

"He's the hoss thief!" shrieked the tramp. "Ask him if he isn't."

The leader, who had him by the collar, paused, and the words of the captive seemed to make some impression on him.

"We don't want to make no mistake," he said. "Mebbe we might ask him."

"You hear what this man says?"

"Yes," answered Walter, in husky accents.

"Is it true? Are you the hoss thief?"

"No!"

Horatio Alger, Jr.

And the poor tramp would have been dragged away, but Walter, his face pale, but resolute, held up his hand to secure attention.

"Listen!" he said. "I am not a horse thief, but I was put here charged with stealing the horse of Colonel Owen."

"Just as I said, gentlemen," chimed in the inebriate.

"Then we've got the wrong one!" said the leader. "Here, you can go!"

"We must have you!" went on the leader, approaching Walter's cell.

"What do you want to do with me?" asked Walter, with sinking heart.

"String you up! That's the way we serve hoss thieves!"

"Gentlemen!" said Walter, "you are making a terrible mistake.

"Didn't you say just now you was the thief?"

"No; I said I was put in here charged with horse-stealing."

An assault was made on the door of his cell, and within three minutes Walter was dragged out.

He began to speak, but was roughly ordered to shut up.

The line of march was resumed, and a quarter of a mile distant they passed through a gate and began the ascent of a hill, at the summit of which was a grove of tall trees. Walter shuddered and his heart sank within him, for he understood only too well what fate was in store for him.

Horatio Alger, Jr.

CHAPTER XXXIV

A TERRIBLE ORDEAL

At the summit of the hill Walter's captors came to a halt.

"Young man," said the leader sternly, "your hours are numbered. Have you anything to say?"

"I have a good deal to say," answered Walter, finding his voice and speaking indignantly. "Even if I were guilty, which I am not, you have no right to condemn me to death untried."

One of the masked men, who had hitherto stood in the background, came forward, and in clear, ringing accents spoke:

"The lad says right. He has not been proved guilty, and I for one believe him innocent."

"I thank God," said Walter, "that there is one among you whose heart is not wholly hardened. I stand here a boy - barely eighteen years old. Is there no one among you who has a son of my age?"

"The boy is right," said another in a deep voice. "Men, we are acting like cowards and brutes."

"So say I!" a third man broke in, and he ranged himself beside the other two.

"This is all folly!" exclaimed the leader angrily. "You men are milksops and chicken-hearted." Walter's face flamed.

"Will you allow this?" he exclaimed, as the leader seized him by the collar and drew him to a tree.

"I won't!" said the first man to pronounce in his favor. "Seth Pendleton, let go your hold!"

"Look out!" cried Pendleton fiercely, "or you may swing, too!"

"You hear what he says," said Walter's friend. "Why are you so hard on the boy?"

"Why am I so hard on horse thieves? I'll tell you. Ten years ago I had a horse that was as dear to me as a brother. One morning I found the stable door open and the horse gone. I followed him, but I never recovered him."

"Who stole him?"

"A man named Dick Ranney, who has since become a noted highwayman."

This was astonishing news to Walter.

"Do you know where Dick Ranney is now?" he asked.

"I heard that he had been captured."

"I am the one who captured him, and for this I received a reward of a thousand dollars!" answered Walter.

CHAPTER XXXV

THE EMPTY JAIL

Walter drew from his pocket a folded paper.

"Read that!" he said.

"MR. WALTER SHERWOOD:

"I have pleasure in sending you the reward for the capture of the noted criminal, Dick Ranney.

"MILES GRAY, Sheriff."

"Shall I tell you the story?" asked Walter.

"Yes! Yes!" exclaimed more than one.

Walter gave an account of the affair in a clear, distinct manner.

"Now, gentlemen," said Walter, as he concluded, "do you believe that I would stoop to steal a horse?"

There were shouts of "No! No!"

And Walter might have gone scot free had he chosen, but he did not choose.

"No, gentlemen," he said, "take me back to the lockup.

"The door is broken!"

"That will make no difference with me. I prefer to stand trial and let my innocence be proved."

"He's a brave lad!" said more than one.

"I wish my John would turn out like him," added one of Walter's original supporters. "You shall go with me, and have the best bed in the house," he continued.

Walter accepted this proposal with thanks.

Of all that had passed during the night Constable Stokes was blissfully unconscious. At an early hour he bent his steps toward the jail. When he saw the door broken he was astounded.

He felt it necessary to report what had happened to some magistrate. He had walked but a few steps when he met Mr. Barry, Walter's lawyer.

"And how is my young client this morning, Stokes?" inquired the lawyer pleasantly.

"Blessed if I know! He's bolted!"

"That is amazing! Let me see how it was done."

"The door was broken from the outside!" he said, after a pause.

"Was it?"

"Of course it was."

"Then you don't think the men could have done it?"

Horatio Alger, Jr.

CHAPTER XXXVI

COLONEL RICHARD OWEN

At this moment a boy of fifteen made his way from the street to the rear entrance. It was Arthur Waters, the son of a jeweler.

"Perhaps I can tell you something about it," he said.

"Last night I heard a noise in the street, and, getting up, I went to the window. I saw a lot of men filing through the street, all wearing masks."

"They must have been in search of the prisoners to lynch them!" said the lawyer, turning pale.

"And you think they broke open the doors, Mr. Barry?"

"Yes."

"And what would they do with the prisoners?"

"Hang them, I fear, without judge or jury."

"I don't mind the man, sir, but I hope the boy escaped."

"Thank you, constable. I am alive and well, as you see."

Both the lawyer and the constable looked up, and there, to their great relief, stood Walter.

"Where did you come from?" asked the lawyer quickly.

Walter told his story, adding: "Constable Stokes, I give myself into your hands."

"Perhaps, as I am his counsel," said the lawyer, I had better take him with me."

"Yes, that will be the best way," said the constable.

Walter was ushered into the office of the lawyer.

At this moment the office door opened, and an old gentleman entered.

The lawyer rose from his seat with alacrity.

"Colonel Owen," he exclaimed, "I am glad to see you."

"Yes, sir. I received your telegram, and came by the first morning train. So the man who stole my horse has been caught?"

"The man who is charged with the theft has been caught," said Mr. Barry.

"Mr. Barry, you have not introduced me to this young gentleman," continued Colonel Owen, eyeing Walter with favor.

"I didn't know that you would care for an introduction," said the lawyer demurely.

"Why not?" asked the old gentleman, opening his eyes in surprise.

"Because he is the horse thief!"

CHAPTER XXXVII

WALTER IS VINDICATED

"Bless my soul!" ejaculated the colonel. "Surely you are joking."

"No, I assure you I am not."

"Then how does it happen that Mr. Sherwood is sitting here in your office instead of being -"

"In the lockup?"

"Yes."

"I was taken to the lockup, Colonel Owen," said Walter, "but about midnight a lynching party broke it open and took me out.

"But I made an appeal to my captors, and was able to prove to them I received a reward not long since for the capture of the famous outlaw, Dick Ranney."

Colonel Owen sank into a chair.

"I never heard the like!" he was heard to say.

"Do you mind telling me, young man, why you were

arrested, or why you fell under suspicion?"

"I was arrested while on the horse's back."

"Ha! But how did that happen?"

"I bought her of a man whom I met on the highway."

"Gentlemen," said the lawyer, "I find that the court is in session and all is ready for the trial."

"By the way, colonel, are you not a graduate of Euclid?" asked the lawyer.

"Yes, sir, and I am proud of the dear old college," rejoined the colonel, warmly.

"I agree with you," said Walter. "I have passed two years in the college."

"Then, young man, here's my hand. My heart is always warm toward a Euclid man -"

"Even if you have to prosecute him for horse-stealing," suggested Lawyer Barry slyly.

"Really, this is very painful!" said the colonel. "I wish I could get rid of it."

"You can say in court that you are convinced of the young man's innocence."

"And I will! And afterward I shall insist on Mr. Sherwood's driving home with me and making me a visit."

Great was the surprise of Mr. Crane and Mr. Penton when they saw the horse thief approach the court room arm in arm with Colonel Owen.

The trial began, and presently Crane and Penton were called on to testify.

"Did you see the prisoner steal the mare?" demanded Barry sharply.

"No, but -"

"It stands to reason that he did, or he wouldn't have had her in his possession."

"Mr. Sherwood, you may take the stand."

Walter gave a brief account of the way in which he became possessed of Bess.

"Does Mr. Sherwood's story seem probable?" now remarked the judge.

"I am convinced that it is true," said the colonel promptly.

The judge saw how matters stood and discharged the prisoner.

"We're left!" said Crane, in a tragic whisper.

"Now, Mr. Sherwood," said the colonel, taking Walter's arm, "you must accompany me to Shelby."

CHAPTER XXXVIII

AN OPENING AT SHELBY

At length they reached Shelby. Colonel Owen lived in a large and handsome mansion with ample grounds.

"Yes," he said, "I have a comfortable home, but my boys are away, and my wife and I feel lonely in this large house. It will brighten us both to have a young face at the table."

How could Walter feel otherwise than pleased. He was charmed with Mrs. Owen.

"I am glad to see you," she said. "May I call you Walter?"

"I wish you would, Mrs. Owen," said Walter.

"Did you find your horse, Richard?" she added.

"Yes, my dear."

"Did you see the man that stole it?"

"Yes, my dear," with a quiet wink at Walter.

"I invited the horse thief to come and make us a visit."

Mrs. Owen certainly was amazed.

"You did!" she ejaculated. "When is he coming?"

"He is here already."

"I don't understand you at all, Richard. You seem to be joking."

"Not at all! There he stands!" and the colonel pointed to Walter.

"What, Walter?"

"Perhaps I had better go to the hotel," suggested Walter.

"No, no! I can't believe anything evil of a young man with your face," said Mrs. Owen. "I am glad my husband brought you home with him."

"I am sure you will both be kind to me," said Walter earnestly, "and I shall appreciate it the more because I have neither father nor mother."

One afternoon Colonel Owen came in radiant.

"Well, Walter," he said, "I've got some work for you to do."

"Mr. Hayward, the teacher of our classical school, is summoned to his home. The question is, Who shall take his place till the end of the school year?

"I have mentioned your name to the trustees, who are ready to accept you on my recommendation."

"There is nothing I should like better," he said, "but do you think I am competent?"

"You ought to be able to teach any of the classes that will come under your charge. How are you in mathematics?"

"I don't think I shall have any difficulty there, sir."

"Then you're better off than I am."

"How much salary shall I receive?" asked Walter, who was beginning to grow interested.

"Twenty-five dollars a week. That's what the trustees authorize me to offer you."

"That will be quite satisfactory. How my old chums will stare when I tell them I am getting twenty-five dollars a week for teaching a classical school. I suppose," added Walter, hesitating, "I ought to look out for a boarding-place."

"What, and leave us?" asked the old lady reproachfully.

"But, Colonel Owen, remember that I shall be earning a good salary."

"You can find a use for it. It will help make up for some of the losses you have incurred. Shall I say you will accept the post?"

"Yes, sir. I will try it, and hope to succeed."

CHAPTER XXXIX

THE NEW MASTER

On the platform of the main schoolroom in the Shelby Classical Institute stood Colonel Owen and Walter Sherwood.

"My young friends," began Colonel Owen, "you are all aware that your respected teacher, Mr. Haywood, is obliged to be absent for the remainder of the term. I have been able to secure as his substitute Mr. Walter Sherwood, who will do his best to carry on the work which Mr. Haywood has so auspiciously commenced. I hope you will receive him cordially and uphold him in his task."

Walter felt some diffidence as he realized what a responsibility had been placed upon him.

He cleared his throat and spoke a few words.

"Colonel Owen has introduced me to you and expressed a hope in which I join him - that you will receive me cordially and uphold me in my work. I will now go about among the seats, make inquiries as to your progress, and arrange the classes."

This short speech made a favorable impression upon

all the pupils with two exceptions. These were the largest scholars - Ben Buffum and Enoch Snow. What they thought of Walter may be gathered from their conversation as they walked home together.

"What do you think of the new master, Ben?" said Enoch.

"I s'pose he'll do. He ought to, if he's been to college; but I'll tell you what, Enoch, it riles me to have a boy of my own age set over me."

"Me ditto!"

"He would do for a primary school, but when it comes to young men like us, I don't like to let people know that he's my teacher."

"It's all right for the others to obey him, but you and I are just as strong as he, and maybe stronger."

"I guess I could floor him in wrestling."

"You're too much for me, Ben, and I think I can stand up to him, and maybe lick him."

"It's likely you can. Now, there was Hayward - he was a big man. I didn't mind obeying him."

"Are you talking about Mr. Sherwood?" asked Harry Howe, a boy of fourteen.

"No, I'm not. I'm talking about Mr. Hayward."

"How do you like the new teacher?"

"He's only a boy. He'll have a hard row to hoe."

"Who'll make it hard for him?"

"Enoch and I."

"Then it will be a shame. He seems to be a perfect gentleman."

"Gentleman! He's only a boy, like ourselves."

"At any rate, he knows enough to teach us."

"That may be, but he can't keep order."

"Why can't he?"

"You'll see whether he can or not," said Ben, significantly.

"Are you going to make trouble?"

"It isn't best for small boys to know too much."

Walter had not failed to notice the half-rebellious demeanor of his two oldest pupils. Moreover, he had been warned by the janitor of the building that they would be likely to give him trouble.

CHAPTER XL.

BEN IS SUBDUED

Ben Buffum was biding his time.

In the seat in front of Ben sat Albert Frost, a much smaller boy.

One day, toward the close of the afternoon, a loud shriek was heard in the neighborhood of Ben Buffum's desk.

Walter looked up and saw Albert in tears.

"What is the matter, Albert?" asked Walter.

"Ben Buffum stuck a pin in my leg," answered the boy. "Is that true, Buffum?" demanded Walter sternly.

"Yes, it is," answered Ben, with provoking calmness.

Walter's temper was stirred, but he asked in his ordinary tones: "Why did you do it?"

"Because I chose," answered Ben.

"Then," said Walter, giving full vent to his scorn, "you are a contemptible coward and brute!

"You forget that in this schoolroom I am the master, and consider it my duty to defend my pupils, even the smallest, from the violence of brutes."

"He'll have to pay for this," he muttered to himself. "I can lick you, Walter!" he said, with an insolent leer.

He had hardly got the words out of his mouth when Walter was upon him. He was wonderfully quick in his movements, whereas Ben, though powerful, was slow, and before he well knew what was going to happen he was dragged by the collar from his seat into the middle of the floor. Walter let go for a minute, and Ben, mad all over, prepared to grasp him in a bearlike hug. A stinging blow in the face convinced him that he had entirely underrated the powers of the teacher. He tried to return the blow, but, unable to defend himself, found his own blow parried and another planted in his chest, causing him to stagger. Then Ben lost all caution, and with a furious cry rushed upon Walter, in hope of throwing him down by wrestling. But, instead, he found himself lying on his back on the floor, looking up at the teacher.

Ben got up slowly and "pitched in" once more, but in about a minute he found himself again in a recumbent position.

"Have you had enough?" asked Walter.

"I hit my head," answered Ben, in a sulky tone.

"I hope you are not seriously hurt," said Walter, quietly. "If you would like to be dismissed now, you may go. I shall be glad to see you back here to-morrow."

Horatio Alger, Jr.

Without a word, but looking intensely mortified, Ben took his hat and slunk out of the room.

When he had gone Walter said: "Scholars, I want to ask of you a favor. Ben is mortified by what has happened. I wish you would all abstain from reminding him of it. In that case the lesson he has received may do him good."

The next day Ben Buffum stayed at home, and did not show himself on the street till evening. When he found that no one spoke to him of the affair he took courage to go to school the day after. Walter overtook him on the way and hailed him in a friendly manner with: "We will forget all about that little affair day before yesterday, Ben. You are pretty strong."

"I couldn't do nothin' against you."

"No, because I have taken lessons in boxing."

"I'd like to box."

"If you'll come round and see me this evening, Ben, I'll give you the first lesson."

The scholars were very much surprised to see Ben and the teacher walking to school together, and were further surprised at the wonderful change for the better that took place in the once rebellious pupil.

CHAPTER XLI

CONCLUSION

Mrs. Deborah Simpkins, a near neighbor of Doctor Mack, was an ill-natured gossip, and had always disliked Walter because he once interfered to prevent a boy of hers from abusing a young companion. One day about two months later she put on her bonnet and with a smile of malicious satisfaction walked over to the doctor's house.

"How do you do, Mrs. Sprague?" she said. "I thought I'd run over and have a chat with you."

"Come in, Mrs. Simpkins," said Nancy, civilly, but not cordially, for she did not like her visitor.

"I've got something unpleasant to tell you," went on the widow, as she sat down in a rocker. "I'm awful sorry."

"Are you?" said Nancy, dryly. "What's it all about?"

"I got a letter from my niece Sophrony, out in Iowa, yesterday, and she sent me a cuttin' from an old paper. It's somethin' awful!"

"Is it?"

Horatio Alger, Jr.

"Yes, and it's about Walter Sherwood!" continued Mrs. Simpkins, triumphantly.

"He hasn't met with an accident, has he?" inquired Nancy, turning pale.

"It's wuss than that!" answered the widow, nodding her head ominously.

"Worse than an accident?"

"Yes; leastways, I call it so."

"Let me hear it, then, Mrs. Simpkins."

"Here 'tis; you can read it for yourself."

This was the paragraph:

"A young man named Walter Sherwood was arrested yesterday, charged with stealing a valuable mare belonging to Colonel Richard Owen. We understand his trial is to take place this morning."

"When is the paper dated?" asked Nancy, who did not appear so much overcome as her visitor expected.

"Over two months since. Walter Sherwood is probably in jail now. I feel for you and the doctor," said Mrs. Simpkins, in a tone far from sympathetic, fixing her beadlike eyes on the housekeeper.

"That's very good of you, but, as we got a letter from Walter yesterday, there ain't no call to be troubled."

"Did he write from the jail?"

"Don't be a fool, Mrs. Simpkins! He wrote from the town of Shelby, where he has been teaching a classic school, and he inclosed the program of the exhibition. Perhaps you would like to look at it."

Mrs. Simpkins took the paper, and looked intensely disappointed as she saw that Nancy had only told the truth.

"He teach school! A boy like him!" she ejaculated.

"Yes, Mrs. Simpkins, and it's been a great success. They want him to go back next year, but the doctor prefers to have him finish out his college course. We're expecting him home every day."

There was a noise heard as of the front door opening, and a moment later Walter was in the room.

"Oh, Walter!" exclaimed Nancy, overjoyed, in her excitement throwing her arms around his neck. "I'm so glad to see you!"

"And I am glad to see you, Nancy, How's my guardian?"

"He's well, and will be home soon."

"Good afternoon, Mrs. Simpkins," said Walter, politely.

"Mrs. Simpkins has just been telling me that you were in jail for horse-stealing," said Nancy. "She is much pleased to find it all a mistake."

Walter laughed.

"I am still more pleased," he remarked. "I find school-teaching much pleasanter."

"I guess I must be goin'," said Mrs. Simpkins, hurriedly.

When Doctor Mack returned he welcomed Walter with a joy not inferior to that of his housekeeper.

"And so you have succeeded?" he said.

"Yes; the trustees of the Shelby Classical School want me to come back, as my predecessor has accepted a position in New York. But I think I had better return to college and finish out my course. I have a thousand dollars saved up, and a little more, and I think with economy I can pay my own way for the remainder of the course."

"It won't be necessary, Walter."

"But, as my property is lost -"

"You must forgive me, Walter, for deceiving you, but you have just as much property as ever - indeed, more, as you only drew one hundred dollars in the past year."

"But, doctor, why, then, did you lead me to think otherwise?"

"It wasn't altogether a falsehood. About a hundred dollars had been lost in an investment, and I made that a pretext for withdrawing you from college. I saw that you were wasting your time and acquiring expensive habits, so I thought the best remedy would be a year of active life, in which you would be thrown upon your own resources."

"You are right, doctor. It has made a man of me. I shall go back to old Euclid and work in earnest. I have been a teacher myself, and I understand what a teacher has a right to expect from his pupils."

"Then my experiment has been a success, and your year of probation has done you good."

"I hope to prove it to you, my dear guardian."

Walter returned to college, and two years later graduated, valedictorian of his class. The money he had earned in his year of probation he devoted to helping the needy members of his class to obtain an education. Gates alone received three hundred dollars, and it saved the poor fellow from leaving college a year before graduation. Walter intends to study law, and it is predicted that he will win success at the bar. For whatever success he may achieve he will be inclined to give the credit to his year of probation.

Choose from Thousands of 1stWorldLibrary Classics By

Adolphus WilliamWard
Aesop
Agatha Christie
Alexander Aaronsohn
Alexander Kielland
Alexandre Dumas
Alfred Gatty
Alfred Ollivant
Alice Duer Miller
Alice Turner Curtis
Alice Dunbar
Ambrose Bierce
Amelia E. Barr
Andrew Lang
Andrew McFarland Davis
Anna Sewell
Annie Besant
Annie Hamilton Donnell
Annie Payson Call
Anton Chekhov
Arnold Bennett
Arthur Conan Doyle
Arthur Ransome
Atticus
B. M. Bower
Basil King
Bayard Taylor
Ben Macomber
Booth Tarkington
Bram Stoker
C. Collodi
C. E. Orr
C. M. Ingleby
Carolyn Wells
Catherine Parr Traill
Charles A. Eastman
Charles Dickens
Charles Dudley Warner
Charles Farrar Browne
Charles Ives
Charles Kingsley
Charles Lathrop Pack
Charles Whibley
Charles Willing Beale
Charlotte M. Braeme
Charlotte M.Yonge
Clair W. Hayes
Clarence Day Jr.
Clarence E. Mulford

Clemence Housman
Confucius
Cornelis DeWitt Wilcox
Cyril Burleigh
D. H. Lawrence
Daniel Defoe
David Garnett
Don Carlos Janes
Donald Keyhole
Dorothy Kilner
Dougan Clark
E. Nesbit
E.P.Roe
E. Phillips Oppenheim
Edgar Allan Poe
Edgar Rice Burroughs
Edith Wharton
Edward J. O'Biren
John Cournos
Edwin L. Arnold
Eleanor Atkins
Elizabeth Cleghorn
Gaskell
Elizabeth Von Arnim
Ellem Key
Emily Dickinson
Erasmus W. Jones
Ernie Howard Pie
Ethel Turner
Ethel Watts Mumford
Eugenie Foa
Eugene Wood
Evelyn Everett-Green
Everard Cotes
F. J. Cross
Federick Austin Ogg
Ferdinand Ossendowski
Francis Bacon
Francis Darwin
Frances Hodgson Burnett
Frank Gee Patchin
Frank Harris
Frank Jewett Mather
Frank L. Packard
Frederick Trevor Hill
Frederick Winslow Taylor
Friedrich Kerst
Friedrich Nietzsche
Fyodor Dostoyevsky

Gabrielle E. Jackson
Garrett P. Serviss
Gaston Leroux
George Ade
Geroge Bernard Shaw
George Ebers
George Eliot
George MacDonald
George Orwell
George Tucker
George W. Cable
George Wharton James
Gertrude Atherton
Grace E. King
Grant Allen
Guillermo A. Sherwell
Gulielma Zollinger
Gustav Flaubert
H. A. Cody
H. B. Irving
H. G. Wells
H. H. Munro
H. Irving Hancock
H. Rider Haggard
H. W. C. Davis
Hamilton Wright Mabie
Hans Christian Andersen
Harold Avery
Harold McGrath
Harriet Beecher Stowe
Harry Houidini
Helent Hunt Jackson
Helen Nicolay
Hendy David Thoreau
Henrik Ibsen
Henry Adams
Henry Ford
Henry Frost
Henry James
Henry Jones Ford
Henry Seton Merriman
Henry Wadsworth
Longfellow
Henry W Longfellow
Herbert A. Giles
Herbert N. Casson
Herman Hesse
Homer
Honore De Balzac

Horace Walpole	Laurence Housman	Robert Lansing
Horatio Alger, Jr.	Leo Tolstoy	Robert Michael Ballantyne
Howard Pyle	Leonid Andreyev	Robert W. Chambers
Howard R. Garis	Lewis Carroll	Rosa Nouchette Carey
Hugh Lofting	Lilian Bell	Ross Kay
Hugh Walpole	Lloyd Osbourne	Rudyard Kipling
Humphry Ward	Louis Tracy	Samuel B. Allison
Ian Maclaren	Louisa May Alcott	Samuel Hopkins Adams
Israel Abrahams	Lucy Fitch Perkins	Sarah Bernhardt
J.G.Austin	Lucy Maud Montgomery	Selma Lagerlof
J. Henri Fabre	Lydia Miller Middleton	Sherwood Anderson
J. M. Barrie	Lyndon Orr	Sigmund Freud
J. Macdonald Oxley	M. H. Adams	Standish O'Grady
J. S. Knowles	Margaret E. Sangster	Stanley Weyman
J. Storer Clouston	Margaret Vandercook	Stella Benson
Jack London	Maria Edgeworth	Stephen Crane
Jacob Abbott	Maria Thompson Daviess	Stewart Edward White
James Allen	Mariano Azuela	Stijn Streuvels
James Lane Allen	Marion Polk Angellotti	Swami Abhedananda
James Andrews	Mark Overton	Swami Parmananda
James Baldwin	Mark Twain	T. S. Ackland
James DeMille	Mary Austin	The Princess Der Ling
James Joyce	Mary Cole	Thomas A. Janvier
James Oliver Curwood	Mary Rowlandson	Thomas A Kempis
James Oppenheim	Mary Wollstonecraft	Thomas Anderton
James Otis	Shelley	Thomas Bailey Aldrich
Jane Austen	Max Beerbohm	Thomas Bulfinch
Jens Peter Jacobsen	Myra Kelly	Thomas De Quincey
Jerome K. Jerome	Nathaniel Hawthrone	Thomas H. Huxley
John Burroughs	O. F. Walton	Thomas Hardy
John F. Kennedy	Oscar Wilde	Thomas More
John Gay	Owen Johnson	Thornton W. Burgess
John Glasworthy	P.G.Wodehouse	U. S. Grant
John Habberton	Paul and Mable Thorn	Valentine Williams
John Joy Bell	Paul G. Tomlinson	Victor Appleton
John Milton	Paul Severing	Virginia Woolf
John Philip Sousa	Peter B. Kyne	Walter Scott
Jonathan Swift	Plato	Washington Irving
Joseph Carey	R. Derby Holmes	Wilbur Lawton
Joseph Conrad	R. L. Stevenson	Wilkie Collins
Joseph Jacobs	Rabindranath Tagore	Willa Cather
Julian Hawthrone	Rahul Alvares	Willard F. Baker
Julies Vernes	Ralph Waldo Emmerson	William Makepeace
Justin Huntly McCarthy	Rene Descartes	Thackeray
Kakuzo Okakura	Rex E. Beach	William W. Walter
Kenneth Grahame	Richard Harding Davis	Winston Churchill
Kate Langley Bosher	Richard Jefferies	Yei Theodora Ozaki
L. A. Abbot	Robert Barr	Young E. Allison
L. T. Meade	Robert Frost	Zane Grey
L. Frank Baum	Robert Gordon Anderson	
Laura Lee Hope	Robert L. Drake